THE
PARATROOPER'S
PRINCESS

THE
PARATROOPER'S
PRINCESS

Horatio Clare

Published by Accent Press Ltd 2016

ISBN 9781783757411

The Quick Reads project in Wales is an initiative coordinated by the Welsh Books Council and supported by the Welsh Government.

Acknowledgements

'Luminary' by R.S. Thomas © Gwydion Thomas.
Every effort has been made to trace and contact copyright holders.
If there are any inadvertent omissions we apologise to those
concerned, and ask that they contact the publisher so that appropriate
acknowledgement or corrections can be made

'Sorry, what?' she shouted.

He leaned towards her, not too close. He was polite but he felt rowdy, because vodka Red Bulls were rushing through him, and because she was very pretty. The music was loud. And she was talking to him, if you could call it talking. She was leaning into him, turning her head so that her ear was near his mouth.

Jase smelled her just before he spoke: a faint smell, delicate, like blossom. In the strobing lights her neck was pale. She wore her hair up. It was either dark blonde or brown.

'I said,' he shouted, '"Where are you from?"'

They swapped positions. He turned his head and bent down so that his ear was nearer her. She stood straight, her mouth close to him, and shouted.

'Wigan!'

They swapped again. They smiled at the pause and the change of places.

'You like them that much?' he asked, smelling her again, and nodding at the band on the stage.

'They're great!' she shouted. 'You a fan?'

He shrugged and grinned.

'Do you dance?' he shouted, after a moment, because he had to say something. She raised an eyebrow at him. She did a little shimmy. He laughed and copied her. They shimmied together, and then they danced. That was how they met. They kissed in the flashing, thundering dark of the dance floor. Her mouth was beautiful. Jase longed to kiss it all night.

1

They left together when the lights came on. In the brightness she was prettier still. Dark blonde hair, that pale neck, and dark eyes, possibly dark green. She wore a black vest and a sort of T-shirt over it which came off her shoulder slightly. Her black skinny jeans ran down to short boots with little heels. The boots were pointed and scuffed. Jase noticed that her toes turned inwards slightly. He loved that. It made him feel tender. He could see no tattoos, no cleavage, which was unusual in TJ's on a Friday night, and only one small piercing in each ear. She had pretty ears.

Jase was wearing the same as most of the lads, a short-sleeved shirt and jeans. It was a warm night, and the rain was fine like spray. Cars sizzled by and the street was ugly, a fast road with chip shops shining, attracting crowds.

'Chips?' she said.

'Yes!'

Jase did not know what else they could do. He could not take her back to his mum's really.

They held hands. He was not sure if she had reached for his or he for hers. Her hands were surprisingly strong, and warm.

'You don't live in Wigan, do you?' he asked her, in the chip-shop queue.

She shook her head. 'London,' she said. 'Where do you live?'

'Nowhere,' he said. 'My mum lives here, but I travel for work.'

'Are you a truck driver?' she asked.

'Not really,' he said.

'Sailor?'

'Close.'

'Pilot?'

'Closer!'

She touched the tattoo on his right arm.

'You're a soldier,' she said. 'That's your regiment?'

'Paratrooper,' he nodded. 'But we're not like any old soldiers.'

'How are you different?'

She had a lovely quiet voice, soft as the rain, and the faintest hint of a northern accent.

'We can fly,' he said. 'Haddock or cod?'

The old lady who served their food smiled at them with knowing amusement. Jase reckoned she had been listening to their conversation, through all the noise of the chippy.

'There you are, love,' she said, handing over the two hot, heavy paper parcels. 'Have a good night. Mind how you go now.'

Now they were outside. Where to eat? There was nowhere nice to sit.

'Are you with friends?' Jase asked her.

'No. I'm staying there.'

He followed her nod to a tall building with HOTEL written on it in green lights.

'That's handy!' he said. He felt a bit silly.

She was looking at him. She was not smiling but her eyes were full of fun.

'Do you know my favourite way to eat fish and chips?' she asked.

'What's that?'

'In the bath,' she said.

Jase had no idea where he was when he woke up. It was quiet. He was in a large bed. His arms were wrapped around someone. A girl. A woman. She had soft, creamy skin, and it all came back to him now. The most beautiful thing had happened to him last night. He could not remember falling asleep. She had amazing skin. He remembered the tan lines around her hips. He moved the duvet to look again and she stirred. She turned her head as though looking over her shoulder but she did not open her eyes.

'Hello?' she said. 'Who's there?'

3

'No one really,' Jase said. 'Just looking. Room service. Making sure you're ok.'

'I'm very ok, thank you,' she said, and wriggled against him.

My God, Jase thought, I must have hit an IED and been blown to heaven.

About an hour later Jase went to the bathroom. When he came back she was watching him. They both grinned.

'I don't believe we've been introduced,' Jase said.

'Charlie,' she said, and held out her hand. 'How do you do?'

He took her hand, turned it over and kissed it. 'Jase,' he said. 'I do very well thank you, Charlie. Great to meet you. Amazing to meet you, in fact.'

Gently he leaned over and kissed her mouth.

He made them both tea.

'What the hell were you doing in TJ's?' he said, when he had given her a cup.

'Working,' she said.

Jase sat near her on the bed. He had a towel around his waist.

'DJ?'

'Very good!' she said. 'I was. Still do a bit. But not last night.'

'Glass collecting?'

'Not really, no,' she said.

'You're not a journalist?' he said, suddenly.

'Why am I not?'

'You can't be! You're too beautiful.'

'Why thank you,' she said, looking down. He remembered last night when he told her she was pretty – the prettiest, most beautiful thing he had ever seen – she had looked away. She did not do compliments, clearly. 'Can't journalists be beautiful?'

'I just don't think you are one,' he said, but he had a strange unhappy feeling.

'Well, I guess I'm not much of a journalist now,' she said.

4

'I'm a writer.'

Jase tried to hide his despair. A writer from London. It could not be worse.

'A writer,' he said, his heart sinking past his boots and through the floor. 'Books?'

'Yes,' she said. 'Books, magazines, papers, radio, plays – all sorts.'

'Why are you a writer?' he demanded, before he could stop himself.

She looked at him steadily. Her eyes were dark green and he could see in them how clever she was.

'Why am I a writer? I am a writer because – I love words. And books. And poems. And songs. And paratroopers, possibly.'

'Do you know any?'

'Only one.'

'Moron is he?' Jase asked, gloomily.

'Oh no,' she said. 'Quite the opposite, I'd say.'

Eleven o'clock came too quickly. Jase had to go. He needed to be at work by two and he had to see his mum first, and get his gear. He had a quick shower and dressed. She was still in bed, tapping away on her phone.

'Are you off back to London?' he asked.

She looked up and nodded.

'Do you think you'll come back to Wales?'

She nodded again, slowly, holding his eye. 'Will you ever come to London?' she asked.

'I might. To see you I would.'

'I would come to Wales to see you,' she said.

'Great! When?'

'I don't know,' she said. 'What's your email address?'

'Don't have one.'

'Do you do Facebook?'

'No.'

'Instagram?'

'No.'

'Carrier pigeons? Radios? What do paratroopers use?'

'We don't tell you we're coming.'

'How will you find me?'

'Telephone?'

'Ok,' she said. 'There's a pad and a pen there. Write your name, rank and telephone number and I'll tell you mine.'

'Here's a better idea,' said Jase. He recited his number and she put it into her phone.

'Call me now,' he said, 'then I'll have yours.'

'Are we going to swap names too, or don't we know each other well enough yet?'

'Lewis,' Jase said. 'Colour Sergeant Jason Lewis, B Company, First Battalion, Parachute Regiment, at your service, ma'am,' and he gave her a perfect salute, his back as straight as a sword.

'Wow,' she said. 'Don't you ever do that to me in uniform. I'll faint.'

They kissed. She still tasted like flowers, Jase thought. And tea.

'What's your surname, Charlie?'

'It's Weston, Colour Sergeant,' she said. 'Charlie Molly Weston, but please don't google me. You'll only find out what a lousy journalist I really am.'

'I won't,' Jase said, 'I promise you that.'

After he had seen his mother and promised to look after himself and call her soon, Jase loaded his bag into the car and set off. He was based at St Athan, to the west of Cardiff, but this weekend he was on exercise in the Brecon Beacons with the boys from Hereford. He had two hours to make the base at Credenhill. Plenty of time.

It was a spring day and the border country was coming out in all its colour. He took the road to Monmouth first, but turned off at Raglan for Abergavenny, knowing it was an easy and pleasant route from there on. The radio played and he turned it up and sang along to the tunes he knew. His mind was full of her, and last night.

But his happiness was shadowed by his secret. He did not think she had guessed. It had been a bad moment when she told him to write his details on the pad.

Jase was a very successful soldier. He had been decorated by his country for his service in Afghanistan. He was liked and respected by the men and women he worked with, and marked out by his senior officers for a serious career in a serious part of the armed forces. His battalion, 1 Para, was part of the Special Forces Support Group. His Commanding Officer was taking an interest in Jase, and had twice encouraged him to apply for the Special Air Service's Selection Course. If he was successful, and Jase's CO thought he would be, Jase would be drafted into 22 SAS, perhaps the most prestigious regiment in the world.

Jase had not applied. He said he was happy where he was, but that was not the reason. It was not that he was afraid of the notoriously difficult physical tests of Selection, or of the shame, should he fail. It was much simpler than that. Where he was, Jase could manage just fine. The problem was his secret. If he applied for anything beyond his current role, the secret would be exposed, and Jase would rather face any enemy on the planet than that.

It was a very simple secret. Charlie Molly Weston would not have believed it, but if he was not very careful she was certainly clever enough to find it out.

The truth was, although he could manage a few basic words, and he could write his name, of course, Colour Sergeant Jason Lewis could neither read nor write. That he had come so far in the forces was a tribute to his cunning, his bravery, and the loyalty of the one person he trusted, Corporal Graham 'Chalky' White.

As his heart sang with memories of last night and this morning, and his head whirled with thoughts of seeing Charlie again, a tight feeling in his stomach told him it was rotten luck,

7

really stinking rotten luck, that he had fallen for a woman who loved the one thing he really hated.

Words.

Place: Credenhill, Herefordshire
Date: April 25th (Saturday)
Time: 1350

'Alright, who is she?'

Chalky had a way of looking at you which said he knew the answer already.

Jase laughed. 'I don't know! Charlie. A journalist. Lives in London. Ridiculously beautiful.'

'Oh dear,' said Chalky.

'Gets worse,' Jase said. 'She loves "words", she says.'

'Oh dear, oh dear,' said Chalky.

'But you should see her! She is lovely. Lovely. Amazing. Really amazing.'

'Lovely, lovely, amazing, amazing,' Chalky said slowly. 'Oh dearie me.'

They were waiting by the truck for Captain Williams. The platoon were all squeezed into the back and they were not happy about it. When the Captain appeared the three men climbed into the cab. Chalky drove.

The Captain burbled away about how much he liked coming to Credenhill. He said one of the best things about being in the Special Forces Support Group was the chance to use all the various weapons from around the world with which the SAS trained. He said he liked days like this, at their ranges, when every member of the platoon would fire more bullets in two hours than most British soldiers would use in a year.

Chalky made the right noises, agreeing with the Captain, and Jase daydreamed about Charlie.

'Want a competition, Colour?' Captain Williams asked.

9

'Your section against Chalky's, and I'll take the third? Losers buy drinks for the other two?'

'He's in love,' Chalky said. 'He won't be able to hit a barn today.'

'Who is she?' Williams demanded.

'A journalist, from London,' Chalky put in.

'Oh dear,' Williams said. 'I bet you haven't had two hours' sleep.'

Jase all but blushed.

Two hours later they were finished. Jase had shot well. Chalky, as usual, had shot better. The instructors had complimented Captain Williams on the platoon's overall standard. Everyone was happy. But as they drove back to the lines the windscreen caught the first spots of rain.

'Rain and wind forecast,' the Captain said. 'It's going to be Baltic tonight. RV at 2100 at Storey Arms. Make sure they know what they're in for.'

'Right,' said Jase.

That night the platoon was playing the part of 'Hunter Force'. The latest batch of SAS recruits, those who had passed the Winter Selection Course, were now being tested on their escape and evasion skills. Last night they had been dropped off at different places around the Brecon Beacons and told to find their way to a certain location without being caught. All night and throughout the day another platoon had been hunting them. Now Jase, Chalky and Captain Williams were going to take over. Their job was to finish the hunt for any of the recruits who had not been caught already.

Place: Western Brecon Beacons
Date: April 26th (Sunday)
Time: 0347

'Sod this for a game of soldiers,' Chalky said quietly. 'It's lucky we're so overpaid.'

The wind was blowing the rain horizontally through the dark. The temperature could not have been more than two degrees centigrade: add the wind chill and the night was freezing.

Half the platoon was making a sweep through a stand of tangled fir trees, led by Captain Williams. In the valley below them was the little cottage, owned by the army, which was the target for the three recruits who were still out there somewhere in the darkness.

The fir trees offered obvious cover for anyone trying to sneak up on the cottage. Chalky and Jase had led 'Hunter Force' exercises before. They always caught someone in the trees.

The two friends were with the other half of the platoon now, just below the firs, waiting for anyone who was hiding in them to break cover. Their men were close around them, concealed and silent.

'Bet you wish you were eating chips in the bath with Miss Shakespeare.'

(Jase had told Chalky, in confidence, about the most unusual and delicious come-on line he had ever heard.)

'No, no. I'd much rather be here with you, Corporal. I wish this night would last forever.'

'You're serious about this girl then?'

Jase did not answer.

'Think she's the one, or another one?'

11

Jase did not answer.

'Oh dear,' Chalky said. 'Oh dear, oh dear. You do think she's the one and you're bricking it. A writer! Your poor, poor bastard.'

Jase knew Chalky couldn't see him smiling, but he also knew he could sense it. He wondered how much of his deeper fear Chalky could also sense.

'Look, we've beaten the army, right? We beat school, recruitment, P Company, all those tests, and then we beat blimmin' Afghan. How hard can this woman be?'

'Hard,' Jase said. 'She left a message on my phone.'

'What?'

'Do I want to go to a gig with her in Cardiff on Friday.'

'Great! You're in!'

'She's going to find out. You know what women are like. And she's super smart, isn't she?'

'Jase, you are going to have to tell someone, because as we know I am the worst reading-and-writing teacher on earth.'

'The worst in the entire universe,' Jase put in.

'Yeah well, can't make peaches out of pigs. The point is, she'll teach you. Who better? You can have your lessons in the bath or the sink or wherever.'

Jase smiled. 'Yeah, maybe,' he said, but in his heart he felt darkness.

Jase more sensed than saw the movement, low to his right, fewer than fifty metres away.

'Two o'clock,' he hissed, 'corner of the wood!'

'Got it,' Chalky said, and was gone, moving quickly, very low.

They did not have to say more. If there was more than one man hiding in the wood, the kerfuffle of the first being caught would be a perfect moment for the second to make a break. Jase would cover that possibility.

Seconds passed. There was no danger here, but the battle clock was running in Jase's head, time passing at half speed, his

12

vision sharpened, heart rate up. These were the moments when you had to make yourself think twice as clearly, so as not to be swept along by events you should be directing. Chalky would wait until the last second before switching on the powerful torch. Jase must not look that way when the light came on or he would lose his night vision. At the same time, he needed to be sure Chalky really had the man and did not need back-up. It was more like rugby in the dark than war, but letting a target escape would be serious.

Chalky shouted, 'Stay where you are!' and the light came on. Jase forced himself to look away, to scan the dark edge of the wood.

'Stop or I shoot!' Chalky shouted now, and Jase heard the sound of a rifle being cocked. A nice touch, he thought – they had no ammunition, and would never shoot their own, but anything to put fear into their target was good.

He could not help but look now. Chalky's torch was on the ground, pointing at the tops of the trees and the rain. Nearby three men were fighting almost silently in the dark.

There was no point in concealing his men any longer. Anyone hiding would know roughly where they were.

'Lights on!' Jase shouted, and pointed his torch at the wood. Other lights came on instantly from men on either side of him. Some, he saw, were pointing at the struggle.

'Look to your front!' he shouted, and as he did so saw the tiniest movement to his left and very close, behind a lumpy tussock, the kind the soldiers called 'babies' heads'.

Jase got to his feet at exactly the same moment as the last man they were hunting: a tall man in a greatcoat whose hair was pale in the torchlight. He had been clever, inching his way towards Jase and Chalky's position to take advantage of a gap when his mate was caught. He must have crawled as quietly as a worm but he was off now, leaping over the babies' heads, through the gap between Jase and the next man to his left.

It was a straight race down the steep slope, the tussocks threatening to trip both of them. If Jase lost his footing the man

13

would get through. Another soldier fell almost immediately and cursed. It was one on one. Jase went for it with every shred of his power, a rushing, leaping sprint. The pale man ran like hell, his coat flying behind him. The angle Jase was running at shortened the distance between them but the man was a demon for speed, his long legs pumping. Jase gave it everything in an all-or-nothing burst which brought him just close enough to jump off one of the babies' heads like a diver and tackle the man. He so nearly missed, but his sweeping right hand caught the man's right ankle, knocking it sideways across the back of his other leg and downing him. Jase rose and dived again, square into the man. They went down together.

Jase knew the man would fight. Overpowering him without seriously hurting him was out. The man was tall, powerful and desperate. To escape the 'Hunter Force' was almost impossible. If he could do it the recruit would be a huge step closer to one of the greatest prizes a soldier could win: the pale brown beret with the flaming dagger and the famous motto: Who Dares Wins. So Jase resolved to hang on to him until help arrived.

He locked his arms around the man's knees. The man fought frantically, his fists pounding into Jase's head and body. Adrenaline shielded Jase from most of the pain, but when the man jabbed an elbow in the side of his head Jase saw stars. There was no sign of help. Another elbow. More stars. Where was everyone? Jase clung tight, hunching into the man's body. Now he was being kneed, very hard, in the chest and throat. Sod this. He went slack for a second, limp, and the recruit's assault paused. It was a street fighter's trick. In a rush of movement Jase let go of the man's legs and let fly, driving his fist into the pit of the man's stomach. It was an excellent hit. The man doubled over with a grunt. Jase was on him fast, driving his body sideways and over, going for an arm lock. The punch would have ended the fight for most men but the recruit was still struggling. Now torchlight dazzled them both. Two of Jase's paras came piling in.

Jase pulled himself clear. The recruit was a smart man. He

stopped fighting instantly, saving his strength for the next part of his test: interrogation. Jase did not envy him.

'Where were you two clowns?' he panted.

'We had a bet on you, Colour,' replied Private Stevens, who was working a sack over the recruit's head.

'Thought love might have made you soft,' added Private Coles, tightening a plastic tie around the recruit's wrists.

'It's always good to watch a Legend of the Battalion at work,' Stevens remarked.

'I thought you might have confused him with your intended,' said Coles slyly. He pulled the cuffed and hooded prisoner to his feet. 'Looked like you were having a bit of nookie.'

'Getting married?' said the prisoner, through his hood. 'Congratulations! I hope you'll be very happy.'

'Right!' roared Jase. 'Throw this lippy sod in the truck!'

His ribs, chest, face and head were beginning to throb with pain.

'Wait a minute, mate,' the bouncer said. He put his large hand on Jase's chest.

Jase had feared this would happen.

'It's not what it looks like,' he told the bouncer, 'I'm army. Got it at work.'

'I'm sorry, mate,' the bouncer said, as though he really was, and Jase's heart sank. 'I can't let you in looking like that. It's club policy not to admit people with injuries. When they've healed you'll be welcome.'

Jase knew he was not an encouraging sight. He had a fractured left cheekbone and two colourful black eyes. The bruises had faded from purple to dark green. Jase produced his wallet and flipped out his army ID.

'I'm a Colour Sergeant, Parachute Regiment,' he said. 'We're the good guys. Please?'

'Really sorry, mate. Can't admit you tonight.'

Charlie, who had her arm through Jase's, leaned forward with a card in her hand. It said PRESS.

'I've come from London to review the band for *The Times*,' she said. 'I've been dealing with your head of PR – Laura?'

The bouncer nodded. 'Right,' he said. 'You can come in.'

'Not without him,' she said.

'I can't let him in,' said the bouncer. 'It's not up to me.'

'Wait,' Charlie said, and opened her bag. She produced a pair of yellow sunglasses with giant heart-shaped lenses in sparkly rims. She put them on Jase.

'They're Miu Miu, you know?'

17

The bouncer grinned. 'Make sure he keeps them on all night.'

'I will. Promise!'

'If I catch him not wearing them you're both out. In you go.'

After Charlie had talked them past the ticket booth – obviously they were not paying, since she was press – Jase stopped on the stairs, which were lined with mirrors.

'Oh for God's sake,' he said.

'I've got some very lacy underwear on if you want to go the whole way?' Charlie kept a carefully straight face.

'What are you doing to me?' he cried, and let her lead him down towards the music, both laughing. He felt as though his heart was flying.

Place: St David's Hotel, Cardiff Bay
Date: May 2nd (Saturday)
Time: 0458

She lay with her head on his chest, her hair everywhere. He inhaled her gorgeous smell with every breath he took. The pre-dawn light was coming into the room around the tall curtains which were not quite shut. The hotel was the poshest Jase had ever stayed in. Huge room. Massive bed. Windows floor to high ceiling, a balcony with a view of the bay, a minibar more bar than mini, and a gigantic bath where they'd ended up last night – or was it this morning?

Charlie could have been asleep were it not for one hand, which was very slowly stroking his left leg. Jase was more relaxed than he could remember feeling for a very long time. Twenty-nine years, in fact.

'I brought you something,' she said suddenly. She got up and went to her bag. It was a fair stroll to the other side of the room and Jase watched her every step, trying to take in and remember every detail of her, the way she moved, the way her body was.

She came back with a sheet of paper.

'Now,' she said, 'I know paratroopers don't read a lot of poetry, but this is beautiful. And it's Welsh. By R.S. Thomas. Will you read it? It's very short.'

'No,' Jase said. 'You read it.'

'I've read it,' she said, her voice so soft and gentle. 'And I'm from Wigan. It needs your voice. Please. I'd love to hear you read it.'

Jase felt as though a huge crack had just run across the white ceiling high above him.

19

'Go on,' she said. 'Have a look,' and held it out to him.

He glanced down. There were not many words. He looked at the first. It began with L. It was a word he had never seen before. L – U – M... Or maybe he had. Maybe he used it all the time. How did he know?

He pushed the paper away and turned over. He did not want her to see his face.

'Jase?' she said. She sounded bewildered. Or was it disbelief? Had she worked it out? She must have done. To test him like that.

'Jase? Where have you gone?'

Jase did not answer. He felt only rage.

Words, words, words.

When they woke again, May sunlight was flaring around the edges of the curtains and they could hear seagulls squabbling. It was late morning. Breakfast had finished in the restaurant but they had coffee on the terrace. Charlie wore the big sunglasses.

'When will I see you again?' she said quietly.

'I'm not sure,' Jase said, looking at the bay. It was shining.

'Will you come to London?'

Jase said nothing. He shook his head very slightly.

'I'd love to show you a bit of the city,' she said, 'if you come?'

'It's tough, Charlie. We're on standby. Not supposed to stray too far from base.'

'I'm coming back,' she said. 'Second week of June. I'm teaching a course in Pembrokeshire. Five days. Lovely place, near Marloes. I could play truant?'

'What course?'

'The only thing I know,' she said. 'Writing.'

There was a pause.

'What I do must seem pretty silly to you,' she said.

'No, it doesn't. I don't know what you do. You write about bands?'

'I write about all sorts of things. I only sold the piece about

20

last night because I wanted to see you.'

'It was brilliant,' said Jase. 'It was a great night. Thank you.'

'No, thank you,' she said, softly.

They shared a taxi to the station. They kissed goodbye on platform three as the London train came in.

'Will you call me, Jase?' she said.

'Yes,' he said, with a twisty feeling in his stomach.

'I don't think you will,' she said. 'But I don't know why you won't, and I wish you would. Do you want to see me again?'

Jase did not know how to say everything he wanted to say.

'Of course! Of course I do, Charlie.'

She looked at him hard, her eyes searching his. She shook her head with a sad sort of half smile, kissed him hard on the lips, and jumped on the train.

He looked for her through the windows as the train began to roll, but she had disappeared.

The train pulled away as he watched it. Her train. There she was – just inside one of those carriages – and she was going, going, gone. Jase felt a tearing feeling.

He walked out of the station and straight into the nearest pub. He was not due back on the base until midnight, and would not be on duty until 6 a.m. tomorrow. He thought he might do something he almost never did, and get drunk.

After two hours or so it did not seem to be working. He found himself smelling his hands and his shirt to see if he could catch her scent. Suddenly he had a thought, and went into his bag for his phone. He never used it but now he thought there was a chance she might have sent him a message. In the bag was a piece of paper that was not his. He pulled it out. The poem. He smiled. When had she slipped it in?

He smoothed it out on the bar and began to spell out the first word.

L. U. M. I. N. A. R. Y.

Luminary. Like 'luminous', like 'illumination'. Jase knew all about that. You fired illumination rounds from mortars when

21

you wanted to light up the night.

The effort of trying to read exhausted him, as the other words crowded round and swam with bits he recognised and bits he didn't. He folded the paper very carefully and put it in his shirt pocket.

There were no messages on his phone.

Place: MOD St Athan
Date: May 4th (Monday)
Time: 1457

'Said goodbye to her at the station.'

Chalky did not say anything. He waited. The weather was fine and they had had their lunch outside, sitting on a wall behind the mess

'Feel like I blew it,' Jase added. 'I keep thinking about ringing her, but I don't know what I'd say. Sorry, I guess. But that would only make it worse. Make it sound worse.'

'She invited you to London,' Chalky said finally. 'You should go. I'll cover you here. If something goes off you'll just have to pinch a motorbike.'

'Can't.'

'So when are you going to see her again?'

'Don't know.'

'Ask her out next weekend in Cardiff. She'll come up.'

'Feels wrong. I can't afford a hotel like that.'

'She won't care. Posh girls love cheap hotels.'

'Says who?'

'Me. And anyway, she's from Wigan. She can handle it. Go on, ring her. Ask her.'

'Yeah, ok, I will,' Jase said in a rush. He had been playing with his phone. He dialled her, stood up and walked a short distance away from where Chalky sat.

She picked up.

'Hello?'

'Charlie?'

'Jase? Hey – hi! How are you?'

'Good. Great! Great. I'm sorry about–'

'What? You have nothing to be sorry about, do you?'

'I'm sorry about the poem. I found it in my bag. Thank you.'

'Did you read it?'

'No. Not yet. I will.'

'It's only a poem,' she said. 'So what are you doing today? Where are you?'

'At base. St Athan. I've just had lunch. There's a class this afternoon and then we're going for a run.'

'Are you teaching or learning?'

'Instructing.'

'Of course! What are you instructing?'

'The dark arts of war,' Jase said, and managed to make it sound funny. In fact the subject today was silent killing, but he did not think she needed to know that.

'You make it sound sexy,' Charlie said. 'But I'm sure it isn't.'

'What are you doing?'

'Hard labour,' she said. 'Writing a review of a band I didn't really see because I was too busy kissing a gorgeous paratrooper in rather fine sunglasses against the back wall.'

'Ah,' Jase said. 'Well, they had the drums turned up too high, the bassist was hopeless even for a bassist, and the lead singer was on drugs, I think. If you need detail on any of the songs I can help. I didn't miss a second.'

'Pig!' she cried, and they were laughing.

When they stopped she didn't say anything.

'So,' he said.

'So...?'

God, he did love her voice. 'So am I going to see you again?' he asked.

'What about that week in Pembrokeshire? You will meet me then, won't you? If you can? We get the Wednesday afternoon off, and finish Saturday morning.'

'I'd love to,' Jase said. 'Ring me when you get there. Or I'll call you.'

They fell silent. They listened to each other's silence. He

thought he could hear her beautiful smile.

'Bye Charlie,' he said quietly.

'Bye,' she said.

He was right. She was smiling. They hung up. He felt like punching the air.

Chalky watched him walk back. Chalky said, 'Christ. All these years and I didn't know you could smile.'

Jase felt fantastic for the rest of the day, and the night, and he woke up happy. But by the next afternoon he was beginning to worry.

They were in the sports hall with the platoon.

'Not like that, Morris!' Jase roared at one of the men. 'You're not giving him a bloody kiss on the ear. It's got to be one movement, the arm goes round the neck and the knife in at the base of the skull as you pull him down and back onto it. The way you're doing it he's told all his mates and they've shot you. Do it again and get it right.'

'Yes Colour!' Morris shouted. 'I'm just feeling a bit bad about sneaking up on him.'

'Lower, Stevens!' roared Chalky. 'Much lower! Approach below his eye-line or he'll have you.'

'Yes Corporal,' Stevens said. 'It's just I've seen this dozy bugger on watch, you know? Sleeps on his feet most of the time.'

'Knock it off!' Chalky snapped.

'I've been thinking,' Jase spoke to Chalky quietly. 'If I don't go to London, which I am not going to do, all we'll have is hotels. It's not enough.'

'Not enough?' Chalky looked amazed. 'You've got this hot posh London bird running to see you every other week and that's not enough?'

'I want to spend time with her. Proper time.'

'So take some leave.'

'Yeah, I will. But then what? It's a bit soon to be taking her back to Mum. And Maindee is not the most romantic spot.'

'So go on her course. Book yourself a place. Better, Stevens!' Chalky shouted. 'Much better. Alright Coles, now you try it on him.'

'Chalky, it's a writing course!'

'Yeah whatever, doesn't matter. You're paying. You can just sit there and say you couldn't think of anything. Or you can say you'd prefer not to share it. Tell 'em it's classified. It's not like bloody school.'

'But they're going to want to see something, aren't they?'

'If they do I'll write it for you,' Chalky said. 'Now stop moaning. We'll book you on this evening. Do you know when I last had my oats with a posh bird? About a decade ago. Do you know when I last had my oats at all? Three months, two weeks, one day and sixteen hours.'

'Bad luck, Corporal!' shouted Stevens, who had crept up behind the two friends, bent double, below their eye-lines. 'Was it a man or a sheep?'

Place: Tŷ Croes Writers' Centre,
       Marloes, Pembrokeshire
Date: June 11th (Monday)
Time: 1553

Jase felt properly nervous as he followed the P signs to the car park. It was a farmyard, but the barns had all been converted Jane reversed into the space so that the car was pointing outwards, ready to go. It was a habit that the army had given him, like never walking on the skyline, always making his bed perfectly in the morning, keeping everything neat and everything clean.

Inside the farmhouse the entrance hall was hung with pictures, old posters and photos. There was an office to his left. He went in. A young woman looked up at him and smiled.

'Hello!' she said. She was blonde and perfectly made up. Her accent was from north Wales. 'Are you on the course? Is it Mr Lewis? I'm Eluned.'

'Hello there,' said Jase. 'Call me Jase.'

He shook hands with her and she led the way down the hall, up the stairs to a landing, past a huge bookcase and to a door which she opened. His bedroom was lovely. It was very big, and at the corner of the building, with windows in two walls. Fields curved to a near horizon. The feeling of the sea was all around. Below one window there was a big old desk and a chair.

'It's beautiful!' Jase said.

'It is!' Eluned agreed. 'Like a country-house hotel, some people say! There are ten of you on the course. Most of the others haven't arrived yet. You might see one or two wandering around. Dinner time is seven o'clock, and you can meet everyone then if you haven't already. After dinner there's a short meeting with the tutors to talk about the week, and that's it really. Just to say – this is your week, it's all about you, and we hope you will have a wonderful time. And get some good writing done!'

He called Chalky from the field behind the house. He could see the sea on both sides from where he stood, a couple of fields away to the south, and a short distance below the road on the north side. Tŷ Croes stood half way down the Marloes Peninsula. On this June afternoon it was like paradise.

'Radio check, over,' he said.

'Loud and clear,' came Chalky's voice. 'Do you have visual on the target, over?'

'Negative,' Jase said. 'It's a bloody lovely place though, and there's a girl here for you – the future Mrs White, I reckon. Name Eluned. Blonde, five-five, one of those perfect tidy ones, sounds like she's from Dolgellau or somewhere, over.'

'Roger that! Correction, do NOT roger that. Observe and report. Where's yours?'

'Still not arrived,' Jase said.

'Bloody writers,' Chalky said. 'Posh birds. Always late. Any sign of the enemy?'

'Negative. How are the boys?'

'Shambles,' Chalky said. 'Did river-crossing drills this morning. And the Major was there, wasn't he? Useless sods, the lot of them. Just about got away with it.'

'Good work, Corporal!'

'Sod off, Shakespeare,' said Chalky. 'Go write me a poem.'

She wasn't there at the start of dinner. He sat with the nine other course members – four men and five women – around the long table, eating lasagne and salad, drinking wine, and talking. Eluned was there, too. She sat next to Jase. On the other side of her was another tutor, Tommy Rees. His age was hard to guess, late forties at least. He wore a big tweed cap pushed back on his

28

head, and small spectacles. His accent was pure Manchester, but he talked about Wales a lot. Jase liked the look of him. Tommy seemed like he had lived. The other people on the course talked about his books – they all seemed to have read them. Full of sex and drugs and violence, apparently, which sounded reasonable to Jase, but also with 'a real poet's sensibility', according to the woman sitting next to him. Jase was not sure what that meant.

'Has the other tutor not arrived yet?' the woman asked Tommy.

'Charlie? No. She's coming from London – must take blooming ages.'

Jase felt as nervous as if he was waiting for the go on an op. He had not spoken to her since that last call, weeks ago. She did not know he was here. He had discussed it with Chalky. If she was not happy to see him he would go immediately, and that would be that. But if she was...

He felt so excited at the thought that he had no appetite and he was drinking more wine than he ever did. He was a beer man, normally.

Jase was in the kitchen, clearing away the remains of the lasagne, when he heard the soft sound of Charlie's voice next door. His heart jumped. He put the dirty plates and the cutlery carefully in the dishwasher. Then he ran his hands under the tap, wiped them on a tea towel, and headed back. His pulse was going strong. He felt like singing.

Charlie was wearing a short dark coat and an Indiana Jones hat with a wide brim. She had a big leather travelling bag Jase recognised. Eluned was talking to her and Charlie was nodding and smiling, and taking in the people in the room. Red lipstick, Jase saw, and her hair was up under the hat. As he came down the two steps into the dining room her eyes flickered towards him and her gaze met his.

He smiled. Her eyes widened for a second and just for that instant Jase's stomach tightened – uh-oh, he thought, here goes! But then, with the tiniest look which she shot right at him, her face lit with a huge smile which she turned on Eluned. And her cheeks took on the smallest tinge of pink, Jase saw, and she was laughing at something Eluned said. Oh yes, he thought, yes, yes, yes!

He spoke to her a few minutes later. Everyone else was eating chocolate sponge, as he set her food down.

'Oh!' she said. 'Thank you so much.' Her dark green eyes shone.

'Pleasure,' he said.

'This is Jase,' said Eluned. 'Jase, this is Charlie, obviously.'

'Hi!' said Charlie.

She said it with amusement and a kind of surprise, which made him smile, because she had said the same thing to him in exactly that way when coming back from the bathroom, naked, in the first hotel, and climbing into bed.

'Hi,' he said. 'Long journey?'

'A bit,' she said. 'And my sat nav got lost. And I had a puncture outside Oxford.'

'Your sat nav got lost?'

'I know! Maybe a comet hit the satellite, do you think?'

'Must have,' said Jase.

Tommy Rees, who was sitting next to Charlie, leaned back. 'A comet hit the satellite! I like that! Do you find that comet follows you around? You must be like Genghis Khan to satellites.'

'Everywhere I go,' she said. 'It's amazing. Sat navs crash, satellites fall like snow.'

Eluned said, 'Jase is in the army. You probably never get lost, do you?'

'The trick is never to admit it,' Jase said. 'We call it tactical reconnaissance.'

'Tactical reconnaissance!' Tommy said, filling first Charlie's wine glass, and then his own again. 'I like that! I might nick that, actually.'

'Be my guest,' said Jase. 'We would probably call that "intelligence sharing".'

'Brilliant!' said Tommy.

When supper was cleared away they all moved into the drawing room, where many sofas and large chairs allowed them to sit in a wide circle. There was a fire going and most people had more wine.

'Basically, tonight we just want introductions,' Tommy said when everyone had settled. 'And maybe you could tell us a bit about what you hope to get out of the course? Then we'll start at nine-thirty tomorrow. If you sign for tutorials in the afternoons, you get half an hour one-on-one with me and the same with Charlie.'

Charlie just happened to be looking at Jase then, and when their eyes met he could have sworn he saw a flash of pure mischief.

'And then tomorrow night Charlie and I will do a short reading, then there's the guest reader on Wednesday – the poet Andy Mulholland – should be good. Thursday's normally pub night, and Friday you all read something you've written during the week.'

Oh hell, thought Jase. Oh well. Friday's a long way away.

'Charlie?' Tommy continued, 'does that sound right?'

'Sounds perfect,' Charlie said. 'Except – Wednesday afternoon?'

'Ah, yes, yes, Wednesday afternoon! On Wednesday there are no tutorials in the afternoon. Tutors' free afternoon. That's so me and Charlie can get a break, and catch up on our reading.'

'Or sleeping,' Charlie said, and everyone laughed. She added seriously: 'But if you have work that you want us to read for tutorials, let us have it as soon as possible.'

Wednesday afternoon, Jase thought, and every night, and Saturday... Thank you, oh kind, good, lovely God. *Thank you.*

They went round the room, everyone taking turns to tell the group their names, where they were from, and something about why they had come on the course.

31

Jase had an excellent memory. If he went out for a meal with Chalky and some friends, six months later Jase could tell you what everyone had ordered and what the conversations were about and who said what. It was very useful: Jase never forgot a single word of a briefing, or instructions, or any detail of any event he witnessed. He automatically divided the group by their projects.

Three of the women – Hermione, Anthea and Carol – wanted to write about their various travels. He thought that Hermione might be giving him the eye. She had lots of frizzy hair and a cat-like posture, hands together. Late forties, pretty. She looked like trouble, and rich. The woman called Carol was tall and attractive. Younger than Hermione, and she seemed more fragile. She spoke very quietly. Jase's mother would have said she was uncomfortable in her own skin, and she would have taken Carol aside and given her a cup of tea and got her to talk about it. Anthea was the woman who had sat next to him at dinner, and turned out to be a chiropodist from London.

Four of the course members – Winifred, Robin, David and Stephen – wanted to write about themselves: their life stories, or stuff about their families or jobs. Winifred was by far the oldest person there – maybe late seventies – very tall, with white hair and a booming voice like a posh foghorn. She obviously cared nothing for what anyone thought of her and had a deafening but infectious laugh. Robin was a quiet-looking psychiatrist from Cambridge, with flyaway hair and eyes for no one except Hermione (though she never looked at him). David and Stephen were friends, despite David being in his mid-sixties and Stephen being about Jase's own age, and had arrived together in David's huge Bentley, which Jase reckoned was worth more than his Mum's house in Maindee. David was apparently in the music business.

The fifth woman – Laura – wanted to write a lot of things, including children's books. But she'd come on this course, she said, to learn about the whole business of writing books. She was a lawyer from London and her eyes, behind rectangular glasses, were full of fun.

The fourth man, Richard, said he was going to write a bestselling showbiz scandal book. He was an impresario. 'Good money and lots of young actresses,' he said, grinning. 'I've got the material.' He was a tall, handsome man and wore expensive clothes that looked classy without being flattering. His shirt was a bit too tight on him and was buttoned right to the neck. His spotless white cotton trousers were also a bit tight, and he wore very shiny shoes. During the meal he'd seemed very interested in Eluned, but had failed to break into the conversation she had been having with sad Carol. After Richard had described his book, everyone made polite noises, agreeing they would definitely want to read that.

Jase was almost caught out when it was his turn, because he was looking at Charlie's calves, the way they curved and very gently swelled above her short boots, and the way her black leggings clung to them, and what perfect shapes her legs were made of.

'Jase!' said Tommy, with a grin that told Jase Tommy had read his mind.

'Hi, I'm Jase. From Newport. I'm in the army. I'm not a writer and I would like to get better. There's lots of stories in the army, of course. We can't tell half of them. But maybe one day. So mostly I'm just here to listen and learn, if I can.'

'Do you get much time to read, Jase?' Tommy asked.

'None,' Jase answered. 'When you're a private you might, and some of the officers find time, but for the NCOs, people like me, none of us read at all, hardly.'

'There are quite a lot of books being written by soldiers,' Charlie said, 'about Afghanistan and Iraq. And they're popular, aren't they?'

'Good luck to them,' Jase said. 'The last thing I would want to read is anything to do with Afghan!'

'Were you out there?' Tommy asked.

'Two tours,' Jase said.

'But you wouldn't want to write about it?' asked Charlie.

'I don't think about it,' Jase said. 'Point is, normal soldiering is probably quite boring for other people. We make it fun, like we have a laugh, you have to, but when it gets noisy and people start dying it's horror. Like, real horror? Too much. So you deal with that however you can – trying to see it like a really dark cartoon is one way. And then you have to move on. Otherwise you'd lose it.'

There was a moment of silence. Damn, Jase thought, had too much wine, and said too much. Then Tommy Rees said, 'Well, with the stories in this room I reckon we can have a really interesting week.'

'Yup,' said Charlie. 'It's going to be a good one.'

And everyone agreed with that.

The group broke up slowly. Eluned asked everyone to sign up for tutorials and cooking. Jase put his initials, JL, in boxes on the forms. He made sure he got the last slot on Friday with Charlie. We won't get much work done, he thought.

Eluned collected the forms.

'Oh, Jase!' she said. 'You've put yourself down for cooking twice! No, four times! You only have to do it once.'

'I like cooking,' Jase said. 'I'm not much of a writer but at least I can work in the kitchen.'

'You don't have to do that. I'm going to take you off Thursday and put – let's see who hasn't signed – Richard! Richard, you're cooking on Thursday, ok? And who else is missing? Carol, Wednesday, is that ok? You can do two if you really want to, Jase.'

'If I must,' said Richard. 'Would you like a drink?'

'Oh no, thank you,' Eluned replied. 'Got to get home. My boyfriend will be wondering where I am.'

'Right,' said Richard. 'Very good.'

Tommy Rees was piling into the wine. He invited Jase to join him but Charlie had slipped away.

'Think I'll save it for another night,' he said. 'Night

Tommy.'

'Alright mate,' Tommy said. 'Good night!'

As Jase left he noticed Richard was deep in conversation with Hermione.

What next? Jase wondered, back in his room. Obviously we can't be open about it – it will make Charlie look bad. Where is she?

He had the impression the tutors' rooms were not in the main house but in one of the converted buildings across the yard, but he did not know which one.

Just then his phone buzzed. Jase dug it out. A text message. He opened it.

'Hi!' it started, and then there were a load of words. It ended with an 'x' which was good. It was definitely from her, but what was she saying? He looked at the words but they resisted him. They made his eyes hurt. He rang Chalky.

Chalky did not answer.

He studied the message again. Before the x was the word r.o.o.m. and before that a word with lots of letters, Welsh he guessed.

It didn't make sense. He would have to go and find her.

Quietly he went down the stairs. The door to the drawing room was half open. Hermione, on a sofa on the far side, was looking straight at him. He changed course, away from the front door, and headed for the kitchen. It was empty. There was a fire door at the back and he slipped out of that. Now he circled the house in the darkness, perfectly at home. He knew all about moving quietly at night.

There were three lights on in other buildings, two upstairs and one down. He peeked in at the downstairs window. It was a room full of books and computers, empty. The other two lights were in adjoining rooms on the top floor of the converted barn. The only way up was a stone stair running up the side of the building. There was a door at the top. Jase opened it very slowly. Now there were three doors, one left, one right, one ahead with words on it, which was locked. He guessed that her room was one way, Tommy's the other – but which was which? He listened. Nothing. At least he knew Tommy was still in the house.

He tried the left door. It opened. He was looking into a large bedroom. There was a ragged dark jacket thrown on a chair. He closed the door. Outside he heard Tommy shout, 'I'll bring it!' and the front door of the house banged. He knocked urgently on the other door. He could hear Tommy crossing the yard. Jase was about to be caught, apparently attempting to break into a tutor's room. What was the excuse? Quick! Tommy was at the foot of the stone steps, singing 'Fairytale of New York' quite loudly.

In desperation Jase tried the other door. It too was locked. Jase thought for a second and swiftly opened Tommy's door and shut it behind him very carefully. Then he dived under Tommy's bed.

A few moments later the door opened again. He watched Tommy's feet advance into his room. The feet crossed to the far side of the bed. Tommy was still singing The Pogues.

He watched Tommy's hands descend to rifle through a bag which lay under the window. They came out of it with a bottle of whisky.

The feet went back the way they had come. Tommy opened his door. As he did so, and before he shut it, Jase heard the other door open and Charlie's voice say, 'Well – oh!'

There was a moment of silence.

'Hi Charlie!' Tommy said, sounding strange. 'Alright?'

'Hi Tommy,' Charlie said. 'Um, you haven't got any toothpaste, have you?'

'Sure,' said Tommy, 'I have, yeah.'

He came back and got it.

'Thanks so much,' Jase heard her say. 'I'll just – put it back in your bathroom, shall I?'

'Or just smear a bit on your brush?' Tommy said. He sounded amused.

'Right. Thank you.'

A few moments later this was obviously accomplished. Tommy returned his toothpaste to the bathroom and went off down the steps, singing again.

The singing faded. Jase waited a moment and then belly-crawled out from under the bed. He let himself out of Tommy's room and knocked softly on the other door.

'Charlie?'

The door opened a crack. It was dark in the room, but for candlelight. Charlie's right eye peered at him through the crack, then she opened the door wide. She wore a pink bra, tiny pink knickers and nothing else. Her skin seemed to glow gold. She held a toothbrush in one hand, a pea of white toothpaste balanced on the bristles.

'Wow!' said Jase.

Charlie thumped him in the chest. She looked flushed.

'What happened to you?' she cried. 'You bastard!'

'He was coming! I didn't... I wanted to protect your reputation!'

She laughed. 'Where were you?'

'Under his bed. Did you–?'

'Of course! I thought he was you!'

'Lucky guy.'

'I bloody nearly did this,' she cried, and she jumped up and wrapped her arms around his neck and her legs around his waist.

'Take your clothes off,' she ordered him. 'Quickly soldier!'

They kissed as though they had never kissed before.

'Make love to me,' she said. 'Now. Right now. Against the wall.'

'Yes ma'am,' Jase whispered. 'Put down the toothbrush maybe?'

37

At 9 a.m. Jase sat at the breakfast table drinking coffee, his body feeling slow and relaxed, his head in a lazy dream. Their reunion had gone on most of the night. When Charlie fell into a deep sleep Jase still marvelled. His mind was only semi-conscious but with his hands he still stroked her and caressed her, fitting his palms into the shapes of her waist and hips and thighs, in love with the feel of her, amazed at her perfection.

She was not thin, she was not fat. She was toned (she was into some kind of hot yoga) but she was *normal*. A woman with hips and breasts and freckles on her chest and a lovely bum – normal. She was the most beautiful thing he had even seen, or ever touched. He loved her voice. He loved the things she said even at the height of their passion. ('The first time I've ever been taken against a wall successfully,' she had gasped, at one point.) He loved her eyes, the look of mischief in them, and he loved the smell of her hair, and how she was so neat, but how wonderfully the mess and disorder of sex suited her. Her feet and hands, which were not small, but long, he adored. Jase was in love, which he knew was a dangerous place, but he did not care.

Two of the women were talking in the kitchen next door, unaware that he could hear. They were chatting about nothing much and Jase was not really listening until he heard Anthea's voice say, 'I think a certain person shared her bed with someone last night!'

The other voice – Carol's, he realised, not sounding sad at

39

all now, exclaimed, '*Really*? Who?'

'I don't want to spread rumours!' Anthea said. 'But honestly – do you think a good body makes up for everything? Don't you need a brain, too? Or do you go for hunky dimwits?'

'They say the brain is the biggest erogenous zone,' Carol said.

'Yes. I definitely need to be seduced there first,' Anthea said. 'But it seems not everyone does! Guess I'm just jealous. Ridiculously handsome. Maybe you don't care if he talks nonsense if he's really good in bed. You just block your ears and enjoy...'

'You could always put your hand over his mouth,' Carol said. 'Tell me who!'

The back door of the kitchen banged and Jase heard Robin the psychiatrist say good morning.

'Good morning!' cried Anthea and Carol, and soon they were talking about the weather and how they had slept and what fancy teas they liked for breakfast and how much coffee Robin needed before he could think.

Jase downed his coffee and went up to his room. He felt something like hatred for Anthea, and furious dislike for Carol, though he knew she was not to blame. He had to calm himself down if he was going to go through a whole day, a whole week with them. A hunky dimwit! A hunky dimwit who only talks nonsense!

Sometimes when he felt frustrated Jase would go for a ten-mile run, but there was no time before the class, which started in fifteen minutes. Instead he threw himself down and did fifty press-ups, making himself more hunky, though that was not the point. There were no press-ups for the brain, he thought. How dare she call him a dimwit!

Don't get mad, the army taught, stay cool. War is a thinking man's game. If you lose your temper you will be hit for six. You have to out-think the enemy.

As his count reached twenty-five Jase began to feel sick with doubt. Suppose he was a hunky dimwit. He knew he was not, but compared to Charlie... She had been to Oxford, of course. What kind of future was there for a man who could not even read and a woman as smart as that? What happened when she started to get used to him in bed – what then?

He felt cold inside when he finished, which was better than hot anger, anyway. He took a notebook and pen (presents from Chalky) and went down to the library. 'Just remember,' Chalky had said, 'they can't make you do anything. It's not a test. You're paying. Don't be nervous. Have fun!'

'Morning everyone,' Tommy said. 'So today, Charlie's going to lead, and I will lead tomorrow. We're going to begin by describing character. How do you make really convincing characters? That's more than half the battle in a book, I think. For example...'

Tommy talked. People took notes. Jase met Charlie's eye, once, and saw her give a tiny smile. She was perfectly turned out, hair washed, dried, tied back; she looked as though she had slept deeply all night. Tommy seemed fine too, though Jase knew he had not gone to bed until after two, and doubted he had left much whisky undrunk. Jase wondered who he had shared it with – Hermione and Richard?

Richard looked slightly hungover. He sat slumped, staring at his feet. Hermione was pale. Jase looked at Anthea and she gave him a huge smile. You evil cow, he thought, but managed to nod at her and even smile. Don't let the enemy know your strengths, weaknesses or your casualties.

Now Charlie took over.

'So, your first exercise is to describe the room where your character spends most of his or her time. Think about the objects they care about. How does the room smell? What is the atmosphere like? What are the really revealing details? Could be a photograph, an item of clothing... think of Van Gogh's room in Arles. The bed, the towel on the hook, the light from the window – what a strong picture we have of the person who

41

lives there. So, take fifteen minutes and then we'll read them out.'

Jase could not believe it – people started writing straight away! Most of them didn't think about it for even a second.

He had planned to deal with this sort of problem by saying he could not think of anything, or that he had written something that was a bit personal. But now that seemed impossible. Bloody hunky dimwit. What to do? He sat well back, moving his chair away from the circle of tables, and began to make marks on his pad, filling in the lines with squiggles, as though he was writing. No one could see what he was doing. He thought about rooms and people.

After fifteen minutes or so Tommy came back into the room with a cup of coffee. He smelled strongly of cigarettes. Charlie had been typing on her laptop. She had an article to finish, Jase knew.

'Ok?' Tommy said. 'Who wants to start?'

No one did.

'Anthea, have you got something?' Tommy asked.

'I'll get it over with,' she said. 'I'm afraid it's not very good. At least it's short.'

She began to read.

Despite himself, Jase was quite impressed with her piece. It was about a tent, a yurt in Turkmenistan, which sounded as though it belonged to an old farmer. As she described the rugs and old chests and smells and shoes, Jase found himself thinking of a poppy farmer's hut he had searched in Afghan. It was very similar.

Everyone took turns reading out their pieces. Winifred had ignored the exercise and written about two cats: it made people laugh and go, 'Ah, sweet!'

Hermione's was the best, about a kitchen in Greece, whose owner must have been a mad old woman. Richard's was about an actor's dressing room. It was pretty boring, but he read it grandly, as if he was on stage.

After each reading Charlie and Tommy made a few

comments. They were always positive. They said which words and images they liked and made each writer feel good about their work, even when it was not particularly interesting.

Now it was Jase's turn.

He looked down at his squiggles which covered a page in his notebook.

He took a deep breath. He pretended to read:

'This is a small room with cheap furniture. If it burned the fumes would be toxic. There is a window and there are always cars outside. The fire is a fake: gas but it looks like logs. Above the fire there are photos of two men, one old, one young, both in uniform. You can tell the old guy is dead. There is something about the way he looks. You can feel his death in the room, even though it was a long time ago. It is too quiet, even with the cars outside and the TV too loud. On the back of the door is a coat hanging from a peg. It's a woman's coat. It smells of rain. She needs a new coat but she will never get one because he gave it to her. She keeps her TV glasses next to the remote on the arm of the chair, always. The End.'

There was a short silence.

'I really like that,' Tommy said, simply.

Jase felt as though he might blush, because Tommy was not bullshitting.

There was another pause. Charlie seemed to shake herself.

'Great!' she said. 'Thank you. Right! Next is – David?'

David had also described a dressing room, this one for a pop star. It was very good and very funny – it smashed Richard's dressing room to pieces. When he had finished it was coffee break.

Jase found himself in the kitchen making coffee for the group. Everyone was chatty and happy and somehow excited, and Jase realised he was having a good time. People told him how much they liked his work. And Charlie, helping him with the coffees, squeezed his finger as he passed her the milk from the fridge. The fridge was in the pantry, just out of sight of the kitchen.

She slipped him a scrap of paper, raised an eyebrow at him, and went back to the others.

Jase went outside. He called Chalky.

'Come in, Base, this is Jase.'

'Base here. How's it going, Jase, over?'

'It's brilliant!' Jase said. 'But she's just given me a note.'

'Ok, snap and send.'

'Don't you bloody share this!' Jase warned.

'Don't be daft, you daft bugger,' said Chalky.

'Ok, call me right back.'

'Get on with it!'

Jase took a photo of the note and sent it to Chalky.

Chalky rang back immediately.

'Christ on a scrambler,' Chalky said. 'This woman's filthy!'

'What does it say?'

'Not sure you are old enough to know!'

'Come on, Corporal! What?'

'Have you two been at it on a desk?'

'What? No!'

'It says, and I quote, "All I can think of is you taking me on the desk. I want to unbuckle you and ride you."'

'Piss off!'

'Seriously, that's what it says! Now listen, you tell her no more notes. I don't need this, ok? You two can shag each other on the table at every meal but you can leave me out of it, right?'

'Ok!' Jase laughed. 'I'll tell her. How's it going with you?'

'Ambush drills,' Chalky said. 'Like having sex with a beautiful woman for an entire week, except with thirty hairy-arsed Tommies with rifles, in a wood full of psychotic midges, and no woman.'

Jase went for a long run that afternoon, along the coast path, pushing it until the sweat poured off him. He swam in the sea at Marloes Sands, a long, wild beach, with rolling, freezing waves and lots of pale, happy kids jumping into them, squealing. He ran back wet, his shorts and T-shirt drying on him.

Charlie was busy doing tutorials. He did not see her until supper, when he managed to sit near her and fill her glass. She was wearing red lipstick again, because tonight she was performing. 'When in doubt, put on slap, that's my motto,' she had told him. After pudding and coffee the whole group moved to the library, where the tutors were going to give a reading.

Eluned introduced them. Tommy was first. Eluned had printed out a list of his books, and some of the things reviewers had said about him. He had won several prizes and his novels had been translated into twenty-three languages. He was described as one of the most exciting young novelists in Britain, which made Tommy snort, 'Young? I'm practically ninety-seven!' Everyone laughed.

Tommy read some pages about a man whose life, you gradually realised, had been ruined by alcohol and love. When he had finished reading Jase realised he had been clenching his fists while he listened. He clapped hard and long.

Now it was Charlie's turn. She was nervous as Eluned introduced her, Jase could see. Her legs were tightly crossed, the foot of one wrapped around the back of the calf of the other. Eluned used her proper name, Charlotte.

'Charlotte Weston's first novel won the Betty Trask Award, the Somerset Maugham Award and the Faber New Voices Prize. She works for *The Times*, where she writes articles on music, art, fashion, food, culture, books, cars and general features. Her work has been published in the *New York Times*, the *Economist*, the *New Yorker*, the *Washington Post*, and many other newspapers and magazines. And she's a gorgeous woman who we all love!' Eluned finished. 'Please welcome Charlie!'

'Thank you,' said Charlie. She was blushing. She spoke quietly and looked down a lot at the thin sheaf of paper she held.

'I'm just going to read you a quick thing. It's a piece I wrote about leaving Wigan. I thought it might be useful because I don't write much about my own life, but some of you are writing about yours, so … anyway. It's not too long.'

Her reading voice was still quiet. She described leaving the north when she was a student. She described missing her home, the bright fields and the heavy rain, and the food and the way people spoke. She used northern expressions Jase had not heard, like 'peas above sticks', which meant being too big for your boots.

As she read her northern accent became a bit stronger.

Jase drank her in with his eyes, greedily, as he listened. She was wearing her hair up, but little strands escaped at the back, above her pale neck. He looked at the swell of her jumper over her chest, and thought about her breasts, which had freckles on them, he knew. He looked at her long hands as she described the strangeness of London, and missing nights out in Wigan, when girls went out with no coat and tiny dresses, 'the better to flaunt your feathers'. Jase watched her mouth moving and decided that he loved her mouth. He looked at her eyes – she was wearing the glasses she used for reading – and thought that he loved her. Not in a silly way, like feeling soppy about her. He loved her in a mighty way, he thought. He loved her like he wanted to take her home to his mother and stand in a church next to her and tell the world that he was giving up all other women for her, for ever, and then work on the children they would have.

He felt an idiot. Children! Marriage! When she had finished he applauded so hard his hands stung.

Later he sneaked into her room. She was lying in candlelight, barely covered by a sheet. He knelt beside the bed and kissed her hands.

'You're brilliant,' he said. 'You're the most amazing person I have ever met.'

'Shhh, silly!' she said, but she looked very happy.

'I am–'

He could not say it.

'Come,' she said, and pulled him to her bed.

46

Place: Tŷ Croes
Date: June 13th (Wednesday)
Time: 0545

Jase left Charlie's room early but the summer dawn had broken wide, blue and bright. It was quarter to six as he slipped down the stairs and crossed the yard. The trees were busy with birds. Woodpigeons cooed their soft love letters and a buzzard turning high in the air called, once, a mew like a cat. The house was still sleeping. From habit Jase circled it and went in at the back through the kitchen door. As he entered he saw a figure by the sinks, a woman. She cried out in surprise.

'God!' she said, laughing with dissolving fright. 'You gave me such a shock!'

It was Hermione. Her hair was a wild frizz. She wore, as far as Jase could see, only a man's shirt, buttoned low between her breasts. She had been making two cups of tea.

'Sorry,' said Jase. 'You ok?'

'Yes! Been out?'

'Morning walk, checking the sentries,' Jase said.

He did not ask her what she was doing. There was no need. He recognised the shirt as Richard's.

The first topic for the day was dialogue, or 'Making people sound like they might actually be people, not bloody talking puppets', as Tommy put it. He read a bit from a story by a writer called Ron Berry, about men in a coalmine.

'So the first exercise,' Charlie said when he'd finished, 'is to write a dialogue – two people talking to each other. Make them use the language of their worlds, as Tommy said. And make them sound different from each other – no one uses words the

47

same way as anyone else.'

'Yeah,' said Tommy, 'make 'em talk about something that matters to one of them, at least, or have an argument. You can get people to come out of themselves when they mind about something.'

'Ok?' said Charlie. 'Fifteen minutes? As long or as short as you like.'

Tommy was out of his chair like a shot, going for a cigarette and coffee. Charlie opened her laptop. She would carry on writing her article, Jase knew. Everyone else started writing or getting papers and pens ready. Jase's eyes met Hermione's. They both smiled. Then Hermione dropped her gaze quickly and seemed almost to blush. Jase looked around to see what had startled her, and found Richard staring straight at him, looking very odd. Jase could not be bothered to think about him. Richard was crazy. And Jase had had an idea.

Winifred's dialogue had two men talking about a third man. They were saying that this man was an untrustworthy lunatic, but they spoke in code. Not exactly a safe pair of hands, said one. Prone to go off-piste, said the other. Like my second wife during her menopause, said the first. But that's Cabinet ministers for you, sighed the second. Everyone laughed, partly because Winifred found her work very funny, and her laugh was infectious.

Anthea had a woman talking to a camel driver; it was quite funny. Hermione had a Greek layabout trying to seduce a tourist, telling her she was 'photomodel'. David had a Glaswegian father shouting brutally at his son, telling him he would never come to anything. Everyone knew who the son was. Stephen the civil servant wrote a scene in a bar with an older man trying to pick up a younger one. It was very believable.

Now it was Jase's turn. He had rehearsed his piece in his head twice, and covered a page of his notebook with squiggles. He took a deep breath and pretended to read.

48

'Can you hear me, Jimmy? Can you hear me?'

'Yes Sarge. Is it bad?'

'It's ok, Jimmy. Look at me. It's ok.'

'Have I lost my legs, Sarge? Have I?'

'You're going to be fine, Jimmy. Heli on its way. Keep looking at me.'

'Sarge? Me Mum. Will you tell her?'

'Of course I will. You can tell her yourself.'

'Promise, Sarge, you go and see her.'

'I promise. Heli in three minutes, Jimmy, keep looking at me. Eyes open! Don't you dare go to sleep.'

'Sarge, will you tell Gracie? Tell her...'

'What shall I tell her, Jimmy?'

'Just tell her. Promise.'

'I'll tell her.'

'And the boys? You'll tell the boys?'

'I'll tell them, Jimmy. Promise.'

'And Sarge, there's someone else. She's called Sandy.'

'Oh yes? Who is she, Jimmy?'

'Sandy. She's beautiful.'

'Right. Sandy who?'

'Just tell her – promise?'

'I'll tell her. Talk to me about Sandy, Jimmy. What's she look like? Jimmy! Open your eyes! Open your eyes!'

There was a short silence when Jase stopped. Then the clapping started. Tommy started it and everyone joined in. Jase looked at his squiggles and felt his face go hot.

When it stopped there was another silence, then Tommy took his glasses off and rubbed his face.

'Well,' he said, 'bloody hell. Thanks for that, Jase. I think I need a drink.'

Jase glanced at Charlie. She smiled at him, shook her head, and wiped her eyes.

Jase did not join in with the second exercise. He went and helped Eluned prepare salad and quiche and cold cuts and baked

49

potatoes instead.

They had made a date: they were going to go for a walk. Most of the group were going to the beach. It was a lovely afternoon, hot, with a small breeze. The air smelled of warm bracken and peat and salt, and the sky was dazzling blue, filled with sea light.

'Where are you taking me?' Charlie asked.

'You'll see. I've been studying the maps.'

'Of course you have! Umm, my car, or...?'

Jase drove an ageing Mitsubishi Galant. It was not cool, but it was unbreakable, with a big boot, and quick. Charlie was driving a scarlet Citroen DS3 sport convertible, with alloy wheels.

'When you say "your" car...'

'Well, it's Citroen's. I'm reviewing it for the paper.'

'So let's review it.'

She drove very well. Jase found it attractive when a woman could handle a car, but then, he admitted, he found everything about Charlie attractive. He directed her down the lanes to the end of the peninsula, feeling like a king, with the hood down, being driven by this gorgeous girl. At the end of the road a man with a white walrus moustache and a face coloured like a sunset took a pound off them for the carpark. They walked onto the headland, and up to the clifftop, and then followed the cliffs towards the very end of the land.

Two islands lay ahead of them on a shining silver sea, with another away to the south. There were not many people around, but several choughs, which Jase pointed out to Charlie. Black birds with legs and beaks as red as her car, they flew with amazing dives and swoops in the currents around the cliffs, calling 'Chow! Chow!' in voices which sounded friendly.

'I love choughs,' he said. 'They used to say King Arthur's spirit turned into a chough when he died.'

'I didn't know you liked birds,' she said.

'Always,' said Jase. 'My dad was a birdwatcher.'

At first they walked apart. Then Jase found he was holding her hand, and then they were arm in arm.

They found a place where pink flowers, thrift, grew bright on the springy turf of the clifftop, and they lay down there, side by side, their eyes full of sky and sea.

Fulmars and gulls came over, and out at sea there were gannets.

Slowly they began to talk. Charlie talked about her town, and her school, and going to Oxford, and getting a job on *The Times*. She talked about stories and interviews she had done and her whole face lit up with the pleasure of her work and her friends who were writers and photographers and musicians.

Jase listened and laughed and teased her for being a terrible swot. But he felt proud of her, in a foolish way, incredibly proud.

She talked about her parents. Her mother had affairs and her father drank, but they were happy enough. She talked about her sister, a genius scientist who worked in America, and had three kids and a genius husband.

Jase asked her about her love life. Charlie rolled her eyes and described relationships which seemed rather miserable to Jase: one guy who did not like sex, one guy who liked it so much he had dozens of women at once, one guy who broke her heart, and came back, but then she was over him and it was all a mess. She described a one-night stand in America when a guy wanted more nights and she didn't, and famous pop stars propositioning her – one by getting his dick out.

Jase listened, and held her hands, and stroked them. At some point he eased off her shoes and stroked and squeezed her bare feet.

'I love your feet,' he said, without thinking.

'You make me talk so much but you don't tell me anything,' she said. 'Your turn. Tell me about your parents.'

So Jase did. His father was killed in the Falklands, when Jase was seven. He had grown up in Newport, played truant from school and got into trouble.

'I couldn't do the lessons,' he said. 'So I had a choice between being the thick kid or the naughty kid.'

'Why couldn't you do them? You're so clever. You're a phenomenal writer, considering you don't read much.'

Jase took a deep breath. Far away, on the horizon, was a big ship, a tanker. He wished they were both on it.

'I'm really not a reader at all,' he said slowly.

Charlie seemed to digest this, and then said, 'Are you dyslexic?'

'I don't know.'

'If you have trouble reading it's quite likely,' Charlie said. 'Lots of people are. Richard Branson is. Loads of musicians are. It can mean you are very creative. There's a simple test, and you can learn ways to get around it.'

'I don't know,' Jase said. 'I joined the army just short of my seventeenth birthday. It's been my whole life.'

'What about your love life? I told you mine. You're so handsome – women must fall for you in thousands!'

'If only. A few girlfriends. Nobody serious except Samira. Went out with her for two years, on and off, but I didn't see much of her – we were always away. In the end she wanted kids, and a father for them, and we knew it probably wasn't me.'

'And what next?'

'I dunno. My CO wants me to apply for another outfit, but I'm happy where I am.'

'Which outfit?'

'Who's asking?'

'Your lover! Off the record. It's the SAS, isn't it?'

'What makes you say that?'

'I looked up your unit. I think I understand what your role is – supporting the Special Forces? Don't worry. I won't tell a soul.'

She looked so serious, Jase laughed and kissed her.

'I'm happy where I am. I don't need a lot more fighting.'

Charlie paused. Then she said, quietly, 'I'm not sure I believe you. But I'm glad if it's true. I can't bear the thought of you in danger.'

Jase kissed her again. She moved, and kissed him back, hard.

'I'm a Para,' he said gently. 'It's the job. Don't worry, we're quite good at it.'

'That's what scares me.'

'The thought of you walking through rough bits of America for your articles scares me,' Jase said. 'But I trust you to be ok. You're smart. And brave.'

'You are!' she said. 'Your writing is so strong and brave. Afghanistan must have been ... terrible.'

Jase looked at her. She was holding his hands tight.

'Yes,' he said, after a moment. 'It was a bit. But honestly, I just don't think about it. It's the best way – life's what's coming at you. Everything else doesn't exist.'

'You know,' she said, 'if you ever did want to talk about it, I am here for you. I'd never judge you or anything.'

Jase didn't speak.

'Sorry, sorry, sorry,' she said, in a rush. 'I'm an idiot. That sounds so stupid.'

'No,' he said. 'It sounds – very kind. Thank you, Charlie.'

He tickled her nose, very slowly, with a long stem of grass, until she sneezed.

'Ok,' he said. 'A test. I've told you the names of all the birds we've seen. Question one – what's that?'

'A ... greater black-backed gull?'

'Very good! What's that there, on the rock?'

'A shag? Or a cormorant? No, it's a shag, isn't it?'

'Yes. Fancy one?'

'Do I?' she cried. 'I'd almost given up hope!'

She jumped on him, straddled him, and her hands were busy at his belt.

They thought they were going to be late for supper, so Charlie

53

drove them home in minutes, gunning the car on the straights, braking hard before the corners, then accelerating out of them. She had Tom Petty on the stereo and was still singing as she hurtled them into the yard and banged on the brakes.

'See you tonight?' Jase asked.

'After the show,' she said. 'I want to come to your room this time. For your smell.'

'And because you like sneaking around, journalist!' he said.

'True,' she said. 'I'm going to be terribly turned on by the time I knock on your door. Make sure you open it.'

'Unlike some people,' he winked. 'I don't know if I packed my pink thong.'

Place: Tŷ Croes
Date: June 13th (Wednesday night)

The guest reader, Andy Mulholland, was an extremely handsome Scotsman with thick curly dark hair. He was probably a year or two older than Jase. He and Tommy had never met before, but they seemed to get on famously straight away. They each drank, by Jase's reckoning, two bottles of red wine before the meal was halfway done.

In the library afterwards the reading began with Eluned introducing Andy. Eluned was perfectly turned out and made up, as she always was. It was difficult not to conclude, as Andy watched her with a hungry grin, that the poet was stripping her naked in his mind. But he may have just been happy to hear the list of his prizes and successes. It was a pretty impressive list, even if Jase had never heard of any of them. 'Hailed as one of the greatest writers of his generation,' Eluned said, in her lovely north Wales accent, 'and he's not even forty yet!'

'Right,' said Andy. 'First I'm going to read you some poems about war. I went out to Afghanistan and spent some time with the squaddies. I asked them about their lives, and then I wrote this.'

They were very good poems, Jase thought, made from the voices of different soldiers. They brought back the taste of dust, the endless tension, the jokes, the feeling of fear-sick before you went out through the gates to patrol. Some of the lads actually were sick, and Andy had caught that too, and the horrible crack and thump of a bullet passing close by, and the relief of the sound of the helicopter coming to get you out, and the smell of the tents and the feel of sweat beading on your face, and the countdown until you had to go out again.

When he had finished Jase was the first to start clapping and the last to stop. And when Andy read again Jase liked that too – Andy had a plain style, like speech, and it was surprisingly easy to imagine the voice of a beautiful runaway girl, his narrator, rather than a small and quite drunk Scotsman.

When that piece was over they all applauded. Then Winifred got up, said she was tired, and said goodnight. Richard had had 'enough great literature for one day', and said he was turning in too. He gave Hermione an unmistakeable look. Blushing, she stammered something about having a headache, and followed him upstairs.

Jase drifted off slightly as Andy read from his next book. The clapping at the end startled him. Now Andy was signing books for people, and a lot more wine and whisky was being carried into the library, and Eluned was saying goodnight and thank you to Andy. When she had gone Tommy was cracking the windows open, letting in the scents of the summer night, and now sparking a fag, which covered the smells of the fields and the cliffs with the stink of smoke.

Andy had a large glass of whisky and sank into the sofa between Charlie and Carol. He flirted with both of them, gazing into their eyes in turn, topping up their glasses, roaring if they said anything funny, and touching them both a lot. He summoned Laura the lawyer to join them, and poured her a whisky too. Jase, who was quietly sipping a nightcap and joining in a bit, noticed that Carol did not welcome Laura to Andy's little group.

At this moment Richard walked back in. He headed for the whisky. He had time to pour himself one, and ask Andy, 'Are you taking all of them to bed, or just going for a threesome?' when the door crashed open. Hermione stood there, her clothes disordered. She had obviously been crying.

'Richard, can I talk to you please?' she said loudly. Her voice shook.

'Tomorrow,' he said, 'when you've sobered up.'

Hermione strode across the room and took a swing at him, a

full-strength slap which whacked into his cheek with a crack.

'Drunk bitch!' Richard shouted. He grabbed hold of the shoulder of her jumper and drew his arm back. Jase got there just in time, caught him by the wrist, and said, 'Right, that's enough.'

Richard said something very rude to Jase, and Carol unexpectedly rose to her feet and threw herself on Jase, shouting, 'Leave him, you bastard!'

Jase held Carol off with one hand, keeping hold of Richard with the other. Hermione was trying for another shot at Richard and Anthea had joined in, trying to pull her off. Andy was clapping, whistling and hooting, and shouting at Jase to 'let the bitch fight commence!'

Now Tommy came piling in, pulling Carol away. Charlie got hold of Hermione, who burst into tears and dashed out of the room.

Jase released Richard.

Richard put his arm around Carol, picked up a bottle of wine, and led her from the room. Those still in the library listened to their feet going upstairs. Andy drained his whisky and reached for the bottle again. There was not much left.

'Well!' said Laura. 'So this is the writing life, is it? Much more exciting than criminal law!'

'It's like a squaddy night out,' said Jase, 'but with more alcohol.'

Jase had a shower and got into bed. He'd left the others still talking about books. He wondered if Charlie would come. He felt tired and turned off the light, but then could not sleep. The windows were open and the curtains drawn back. He could hear crickets outside, and moonlight came in, making ghostly shapes on the floor and the desk. He lay awake, thinking about Charlie and their afternoon on the cliffs. If they ever lived together, Jase thought, this would be what it was like. Waiting for her to finish conversations he could not join in, at parties he would not enjoy.

At some point he dropped off, and awoke to the noise of voices. Through the open window he heard the front door shutting and the sound of people crossing the yard. Tommy was singing 'Fairytale of New York' again and Andy shouted, 'What a beautiful night! It's perfect!'

He heard Charlie's voice, but could not make out the words. He got out of bed and looked out of the window. A security light came on. He watched Charlie, Tommy and Andy climb the stone stairs up the side of the barn. He saw them go in through the outer door. The guest room was up there, he knew, the third door. Tommy would be going into his room now, and Andy would be making his move on Charlie.

Jase stayed there, watching the outer door, but he could not guess what was happening and he saw no more movement. After a while he went back to bed. He lay, staring at the window, ears straining, for a long time.

Perhaps an hour later the light changed outside. The security light was on again. Jase forced himself to stay where he was. He listened but heard nothing. He was just deciding that a fox or a cat must have tripped it when he heard the slightest sound outside his door. Now the handle turned and the door opened slowly. It was Charlie. He did not say anything. She closed the door behind her, very quietly, and now she moved into the room. She stood in the moonlight and Jase watched her. She slipped off her trainers without undoing them and lifted her T-shirt over her head. Now she undid her jeans, tugged them down and stepped out of them. Now she took off her bra, and her skin glowed like snow in the dark. Now she took off her knickers and came to the bed.

He did not know if she knew he was awake; he thought she did, but something made him keep still and silent. Very gently, she pulled the sheet back. As she bent down to him, her hair fell forward, tickling his stomach.

After a while she moved up and over him, kissing him deeply, holding his hands to her breasts. They did not speak. They communicated through their breathing, and through touch.

58

Slowly at first, then with more urgency, they made love. The climax came with an intensity Jase had never known in his life. He heard her crying out, and himself almost roaring, at its height.

Jase heard a buzzard mewing when he woke. He wondered if it was the same one he had heard the other day. The sky was blue outside, the tone of a hot day beginning. Charlie was lying on her side, smiling at him. He kissed her. Jase looked at his watch on the bedside table.

'O eight hundred hours, Miss Watson.'

'I'm not even going to bother pretending. In fact I am going to cancel this morning. Get me some tea, Colour Sergeant, and make love to me again. Until lunch.'

'Yes ma'am. And then?'

'Take me out for lunch, then back to where we were yesterday.'

'Yes ma'am. And then?'

'We'll do it again.'

'Excellent plan, ma'am!'

'Thank you, Colour Sergeant.'

'How did it go last night?'

'Oh gosh, that man Andy! I had to fight him off!'

'Seriously?'

'Seriously. He put his foot in my door and wouldn't go. I asked him but he kept laughing. I knew if I let the door go he would come in so I just had to keep telling him to go to bed. But he wouldn't! In the end he tried to kiss me, like a proper grab, and he wouldn't take no for an answer, so I hit him.'

'Where?'

'In the face!'

'Nice one,' said Jase. 'What did he do?'

'He looked really shocked, and he shouted "fucking hell!" I thought he was going to hit me but then Tommy shouted out of his room, "Everything all right?" and Andy gave it up. I nearly went mad waiting for him to stop moving around so I could sneak out.'

'Good man, Tommy!'

'He really is. Oh bollocks, we'd better get up.'

Breakfast was entertaining. Tommy informed everyone he had a hangover. Andy had a black eye. Everyone asked him about it. He said he had walked into a cupboard trying to go to the loo. Richard was nowhere to be seen. Carol had chosen to come down with her hair all over the place, in shorts, a thin T-shirt and obviously no bra, and a dreamy smile. She asked twice where Hermione was, but no one had seen her. Charlie appeared ten minutes before the lesson was supposed to begin. Jase grinned at her in admiration. Again she had showered, dried her hair, and possibly applied foundation. She smelled of orange blossom. She was wearing denim shorts and looked immaculate.

At exactly nine-thirty, as they all made their way to the library, Hermione appeared. She was dressed very smartly. She had her suitcase and bag. Her face was pale and tight.

'Can someone take me to the station, please?'

There was a short silence. Jase was the first to react.

'Of course,' he said. 'I'll just get my keys. See you in the carpark?'

'Thank you,' Hermione said, with a weak smile.

'Are you sure you want to...' Anthea began.

'I don't want to talk about it,' Hermione said. She looked at Carol. She shook her head once, turned and walked out of the house. Charlie went after her.

When Jase got to the carpark, Charlie and Hermione were hugging.

'I'm so sorry,' Charlie was saying.

Hermione wiped her eyes. 'It's my silly fault,' she said. 'Say thank you to Tommy for me, he's lovely. And tell Eluned that it wasn't anyone's fault. Really. You're great. I learned loads.'

Charlie told her she would email her, and help her with her book. 'It is going to be bloody great,' Charlie told her. 'You've got it.'

Jase put the case and the bag in the car. He held the door open for Hermione and she got in.

'What a lovely man,' she said to Charlie. 'I'd keep hold of him, if I were you.'

Charlie looked scandalised and delighted. 'You knew!'

'Of course,' said Hermione. 'You told us to pay attention to people, didn't you?'

'What gave us away?'

'You're in love,' Hermione said. 'It's so obvious!'

'Damn,' Charlie murmured, pretending to frown, her cheeks colouring.

Jase did not know what to do, so he got into the car, trying to keep the huge smile off his face.

The drive to Haverfordwest took them along a twisting road. Jase did not say anything, concentrating on his driving until Hermione said, 'Thank goodness that's over. Just to get it out of the way, I am incredibly cross with myself for going to bed with that sleazebag. You don't need to be nice to me.'

'Mistakes happen,' said Jase. 'I'm only sorry I promised Charlie and Tommy I wouldn't let him get slapped until after he's done his feedback form. You gave him a peach.'

Hermione laughed. 'It must happen to him a lot. Maybe his book would be worth reading, just to remember there are men like that out there. I mean, how does he think?'

'Like a seventeen-year-old. A stupid one.'

After a pause Hermione asked, 'So when did you meet Charlie?'

'You don't miss much!'

'I watched you both that first night. She was so happy to see you. It was beautiful. And I saw you sneaking out. And I caught

63

you in the kitchen.'

'Yeah. We met a few months ago. I was at a gig she was reviewing.'

'Are you going to marry her?'

Jase laughed. He did not know what to say.

'Well, are you? You'd be mad not to. You're perfect together.'

'Perfect?' Jase exclaimed. 'She's a writer. An intellectual. And I've never read a book in my life!'

'That,' said Hermione, 'is the only silly thing I've heard you say. What difference does it make? Why does it matter?'

'I'd embarrass her with her friends. Her whole world is not mine. And I'm away all the time.'

'So is she, I expect. As long as you don't ask her to sit at home waiting. Just trust that she loves you. Honestly, I'm good at this. I can tell if a couple works, or if one of them is having an affair, or if it's going to fall down. Ask anyone who knows me. I'm always right.'

'Richard?'

Hermione sighed.

'I wasn't expecting to be humiliated like that. He made me go after him, in front of everyone, you saw. When we got to his room he said we were finished and he was thinking of sleeping with Carol! I said, "You're joking?" He said, "I'm not, but if you want to join in you can".' She shrugged.

Jase digested this. 'I can see why you wanted to hit him again.'

At the station Jase insisted on taking her suitcase to the platform while she bought a ticket. They said goodbye, and Hermione hugged him.

'Marry her,' she said fiercely. 'Marry her, marry her, marry her! You've been given someone incredible. There are second chances, but golden chances only come once. Let her go and you'll regret it.'

'Maybe not today, maybe not tomorrow, but soon and for the rest of my life?' Jase said.

'Exactly! I'm saying it, Humphrey Bogart's saying it. What more do you want?'

'Have you been married?'

'That,' said Hermione, 'is another story. Invite me on your stag do and I'll tell you everything.'

'Bloody hell,' said Jase. 'You're on!'

The train was coming in now.

'You know, Jase,' Hermione said, 'in every great adventure, the hero has to overcome the monster.'

'Right?' said Jase

'So – does she know you can't read?'

Jase just gaped at her. Hermione shook her head.

'Tell her,' she said. 'She'll teach you. She'll love it. So will you.'

He had missed so much of the class that he did not feel bad about skipping the rest of it. Charlie had tutorials in the afternoon so he went for a run, then a swim. He had looked at the others at lunch, trying to work out if anyone else knew what Hermione had guessed. Thankfully, Andy had gone. But Jase felt exposed. He thought Hermione was out of the ordinary but he had a toppling feeling of things changing. It was only a writing course – and who cared what these people thought – but then it was *his* secret, and the thought that even Hermione knew made him shrink inside.

'Pub?' everyone said at dinner. 'Are you coming to the pub?'

They could have got out of it but they could not let Tommy down: he had been looking forward to the pub trip since the first night. Jase felt a blue feeling of time running out and he hoped the pub would be quiet and over quickly. Everyone was going, even Winifred. They organised who was driving and who was getting a lift. Charlie and Jase offered to be taxis, as did David, in his Bentley.

The Horseshoes was two small rooms with a fire in one, a pool table in the other and the bar between them. Three girls and four lads were drinking and playing pool; the writers took the room with the fire. Charlie and Jase moved chairs around, brought tables together, made everyone comfortable.

'What a quaint little place!' Winifred boomed, settling herself by the fire. One of the lads in the next room said something and the others laughed. The first now imitated Winifred's voice, braying loudly, 'Oh spiffing, darling!'

Jase looked across the bar and smiled, to signal they were all friends here, and could take a joke, but then a voice from a person he had not seen killed the smile on his lips.

'Stuck-up bitch,' said the voice, loudly.

There was silence.

A man moved into view on the other side of the bar. He was big, his skin grey. His eyes had a kind of still sheen in them. There was an air about him Jase recognised – of cruelty and violence. You sometimes met men like this in the army. They generally got kicked out and went back to terrorising civvy street. The man looked right at Jase and said, 'What?'

'Easy, Miggsy,' said the barman, and moved to block Jase's view of him. The publican was a large man, early thirties, with a crinkled mane of dark red hair. His eyes, Jase saw, were brown and bright, wise for his years. It must be the writing course that is making me observe people like this, Jase thought.

'What are you having?' said the barman.

Jase began ordering. Richard and Carol joined him. Richard was fondling Carol's bottom with one hand, Jase noted. With the other he banged a stuffed wallet on the bar and said loudly, 'This round on me.'

'Flash bastard,' said the man called Miggsy. The pool lads laughed. Richard looked across at him and prepared to say something – you could see him searching for a cutting comeback.

The barman moved to block Richard's view now and mouthed 'Don't' at him with great emphasis, shaking his head slightly, but Richard sneered, and said, 'Jealous?'

This is all I need, Jase thought.

66

Now Charlie came to the bar to help carry the drinks. Miggsy saw her. His was not a pleasant smile.

'Alright, sexy?' he said, loudly. 'Wanna scratch my back tonight?'

Charlie laughed.

'Get your coat,' she said. 'You've not pulled.'

'You can pull me off any time, darling.'

'Surely you've already pulled it off by yourself, darling?'

At this the barman burst out laughing. It was a loud laugh that took all the attention to him.

'Very good!' he said. Then he turned, 'Another, Miggsy?'

'Yeah,' said the man.

Things quietened down after this. There was a happy half hour, until Richard got up, announced that he was going to have a cigarette, and went out. Jase had been quietly happy, chatting to Laura and playing footsie with Charlie under the table, but now he glanced across the bar, saw Miggsy say something to one of the lads, and all begin to move.

'Bollocks,' he muttered.

'What?' Charlie whispered.

'Back in a sec.'

Jase was on his feet and swerving through the tables to the door.

They had started without him. Richard was struggling with two of the lads who were pinning his arms to the wall of the pub. Miggsy stepped up to him, and as Jase bounded towards them Miggsy said, 'Jealous now, Flashy?' and hit Richard, very hard, in the stomach.

Reasonable force, thought Jase, reasonable force. He punched Miggsy in the kidneys, caught him as he buckled and pushed him hard into the lad on the left. They went down in a heap. The lad on the right swung. Jase caught his arm, ducked under it and pulled the lad forward, using the momentum and a twist of his shoulders to bring the lad over his shoulders in a perfect judo throw. The lad landed hard on his back.

Prioritise threats and neutralise, thought Jase. Miggsy was

up on his knees now. Jase bent, put an armlock around Miggsy's neck and spoke slowly and calmly. Everyone heard him.

'Bruneval, Bréville, Rhine, Arnhem, Primosole Bridge, Goose Green, Wireless Ridge, Mount Longdon, Al-Basra, Forward Operating Base Gibraltar, Helmand Province.'

He twisted Miggsy's neck until there was no more give, and squeezed his throat so that he could not speak.

'We fought men with guns in those places. Not scrotes. At Gibraltar the casualty rate was the same as the trenches. We lost thirteen of ours. We finished two hundred of them.'

The two lads were up now. They stared at Jase in silence. As a Para NCO, Jase had plenty of practice at sounding evil on demand.

'You are going to get your coats and leave. You are not going to speak, you are not going to look at anyone, and if I see you again I will batter the lot of you. Got it?'

Miggsy twitched in what Jase took to be acceptance.

Jase let him go. He went over to Richard. Richard was crouched down, holding his stomach. Jase helped him up.

'Alright?'

'Yes. God. Thank you.'

'Don't mention it.'

'I–'

'Seriously,' said Jase. 'Don't mention it to anyone.'

'Sure,' said Richard. 'Sure, ok. Buy you a drink?'

'I'm driving. Now, smile for the ladies. Nothing's happened.'

Miggsy and his lads had disappeared into another room when they got back inside the pub. But the writing group were muttering and whispering and everyone looked at Jase and Richard as they sat down.

'Are you ok?' Charlie asked.

Jase smiled broadly.

'We're grand!'

In the other bar, Miggsy and the lads and the girls were

leaving. The girls wanted to know what was going on, but the lads shook their heads in silence. The door shut behind them.

Jase met the barman's eye. The barman, with a faint smile, produced a glass and a bottle of Glenlivet. He poured a generous measure.

At this moment Tommy returned from the lavatory.

'What have I missed?' he cried. 'Where's that mad bastard and the rest?'

'It seems they've taken the pledge,' the barman answered. Everyone laughed. The barman cleared the empties from their table. The Glenlivet magically appeared in front of Jase.

'What happened?' Charlie asked later, as they lay in a tangle of sheets.

'Couldn't say. I feel like I've been mauled by some sort of sex leopard.'

Charlie giggled. 'That's nothing. It's your tutorial tomorrow. I am an extremely demanding teacher.'

'I've never looked forward to detention before.'

Charlie raked her nails gently down his chest.

'And what are you going to read at the show?'

'What show?'

'Friday night. Everyone reads a piece they've been working on.'

'I'll think of something. What are you doing this weekend?'

'What are you doing?'

'Asked you first.'

'I am having a dirty weekend in a hotel by the sea. When are you back on duty?'

'Sunday night.'

'Kiss me.'

'Should have joined the army, ma'am. You're officer material.'

Place: Tŷ Croes
Date: June 15th (Friday)

Richard made a huge plate of bacon, eggs, toast, beans and tomatoes and put it down in front of Jase.

'Don't mention it,' he said.

'Oh, cheers.'

'Pleasure,' said Richard.

Charlie gave him a look. He returned one which said, 'Don't ask me!'

She narrowed her eyes at him.

Tommy was also ploughing through a full breakfast.

'Rich made me this an' all,' he said. 'He's a new man.'

David and Stephen came down. David was in a silk dressing gown and carrying a fat cigar.

'Oh, great look!' Charlie cried.

Tommy wolf-whistled.

David smiled. 'I'm on holiday today. It's been so good, I almost have no more questions.'

'Has the week been helpful?' Charlie asked.

'Hugely,' said David. 'A brilliant week.'

Jase said, 'It really has been brilliant. You two have worked your socks off. Great stuff.'

Charlie looked pleased and embarrassed. 'Thanks guys,' she muttered.

Tommy nodded. 'Really enjoyed it myself! Definitely one of the more lively courses I've taught,' he said.

Then Jase's phone rang.

He dragged it out of his jeans. It could only be Chalky or his mum. The last three digits on the screen told him. He jumped up and squeezed past David into the garden, pressing the answer button.

'Chalky?'

'Jase. You alright?'

'I was.'

'Yeah. Sorry brother.'

'What?'

'We're on twenty-four hours.'

'What?'

'Yeah. You'll never guess where we're going.'

'You're kidding.'

'Wish I bloody was. Remember that shithole sandpit? Hot, with loads of mad-heads, and Yanks, and they told us it was all sorted and we could go home? Well, apparently it wasn't sorted at all. And to the left of it there's this other shit pit called Syria, and it's gone tits up there too. And in the middle there's this bunch of Herberts into cutting decent people's heads off on YouTube. So they've asked the boys from Hereford to go and have a word with one or two of them, and guess who gets to watch their backs? This is all hush-hush mind...You still there?'

'No.'

'Really sorry, Jase.'

'Yup. Thanks for the call. How long have I got?'

'You haven't.'

'Alright, I'm coming.'

'Sorry mate. Have you had a good one?'

'Brilliant,' said Jase.

Jase made his face expressionless and headed back in. People were getting ready to go up to the library. Charlie took one look at him and put down her tea.

'Are you ok?'

'Got to go,' said Jase. 'Something's come up, I'm afraid.'

He flicked his eyes from Charlie towards the hall. All the light seemed to have drained from her face.

'What is it?' she said, as soon as they were out of the room and heading for the stairs.

'I'm really sorry,' he said. 'I've been recalled. We're on twenty-four hour standby.'

'For what?'

They were hurrying up the stairs to Jase's room.

'The usual. I'm so sorry.'

In his room Jase ripped his clothes out of the wardrobe and the drawers, tipped them and his wash things into his bag, and looked around to see if he had forgotten anything. He grabbed his car keys, wallet and phone charger.

'Come on,' he said.

They almost ran downstairs, across the yard and round to the carpark.

'No time to say goodbye?'

Jase opened the boot and threw everything in. Then he turned to her.

'Only to you,' he said, softly. 'Say it for me. Tell them I'm sorry I couldn't do it properly. Give Tommy my best. He's gold.'

'You know you really don't have to read anything tonight,' she said. 'You could just pull a sickie. Or say the publishers have put it under embargo. There's no need to be dramatic.'

He laughed. He went to hug her and she threw herself at him, jumping up to wrap her legs around his waist.

'Stay. It's an order.'

'Can't, ma'am.'

'Take me with you.'

'Wish I could, ma'am.'

'Tell me where you're going, at least. You know you can. On my life.'

Jase paused.

'Please,' she whispered. 'I can't not know.'

He took a deep breath. 'Ok. On your life. Chalky said...'

And he told her, word for word.

When he had finished she looked him in the eyes, deep and hard, as if she was searching for something there.

'You know, don't you?'

'What?'

'I – want you.'

'Want you too, babe.'

'That too. But do you know?'

'Yes,' he said, with a rush. 'I think I do.'

'You're going to come back to me, right?'

'Yes ma'am.'

'Promise. Say "I promise I am going to come back to you".'

'I promise I am going to come back to you, Charlie.'

'How long?'

'At the outside, six months. That's a tour.'

She looked shocked, but then she controlled it. She nodded firmly.

'I can be patient. Will you be able to call me?'

'Sure,' he said. 'And there's Skype. But listen, if you don't hear anything it means they're not letting us. It's not bad news. No news is good news. Ok? That's really important. I am coming back.'

'Promise?'

'I already have,' he said gently, and she had her arms around his neck now and she was crying, and now she was kissing him and kissing him.

A few weeks turned into three months, which turned into four, then five, then six. Charlie spent the whole of December willing her phone to ring, and checking it for messages that never came. When January arrived she became convinced that something had happened to him: he had said six months!

She tried to find out something, anything, about where Jase might be, and what might be happening there. She tried the Ministry of Defence and got nowhere. So she contacted someone she only knew a little, a man who had been the newspaper's defence correspondent, and asked for his help. He was a man with a cut-throat reputation, who was said to do anything for a story, to have no friends, and to turn on the charm only for work. Over email he agreed to meet her. He sounded rather cold.

They met in a café near London Bridge. He wore an expensive suit and did not smile. But he listened to her closely. And when she had finished, and was feeling a complete fool, he leaned towards her and his face became gentle.

'If you're not married to him they won't tell you anything,' he said.

'But if he was dead, wouldn't we know? Wouldn't it be in the papers?'

'Very unlikely. Special Forces are covered by a whole different set of rules. With something like this, when they're not supposed to be there anyway, they would tell his next of kin, but they would give no details, not even the country he was in, sometimes, and they would tell them to keep quiet about it. Do you know any of his friends?'

'He only talked about one called Chalky. He was a Corporal.

75

Graham White. That's all I know. And his mother lives in Newport, an area called Maindee. I never met her.'

'Well, she's where you start.'

'I don't know if I can. She didn't know about us, I don't think. And if something has happened … I don't … I mean supposing there's another girlfriend, or a wife or something, and I turn up like this!'

Charlie clenched her nails into her hands because she was not going to cry. She had done enough of that at home by herself, and once with her friend Lorna, when she had let herself go.

'Look, I'll try to find this Corporal White. If I can I'll get him a message. You'd better give me your phone number and your address. They'll want to check you out before they go anywhere near you. And they probably won't, so don't get your hopes up. But you must stop imagining the worst. Those guys can disappear for ages. Half the time they don't even know what country they're in. That's what they sign up for. Britain's dirty business, which all of us are better off not knowing about. And then one day they turn up, tanned and smiling, and they won't tell you anything.'

'That's Jase.'

'He must be quite a guy.'

'He is. Thank you so much. I really … It means a lot. Thank you.'

'Don't worry about it. You'll hear from me. Take care. Find his mother, if you can't bear the waiting.'

'Yeah.'

He stood up to go. She stood up. And then he touched her very lightly on the arm and said, 'You know, you should get in touch with her.'

Charlie nodded but she could not speak.

She decided to give it two more weeks. But only two days later her telephone rang. It was a number she did not recognise.

'Hello?' she said.

76

'Hello, is that Charlie?' said a Welsh voice. For a split second she thought it was him.

'Yes. Who is this?'

'I'm a friend of a friend. I've got a message for you. Can we meet?'

'Of course, yes! Where, when? How is he?'

'Best not over the phone. If you're at home I think I might be down the road, in the Dolphin? I was in the area, like...'

'I'm coming!' she said. 'Stay there!'

Charlie grabbed her keys and dashed out. It was the first time in her life, she thought, she had ever left the flat without the merest pause for anything. She did not quite run down the road. She said, over and over, please don't let him be dead. Please don't let him be dead. Please don't let him...

The Dolphin was empty, as it often was, except for the landlord and a man who stood up as soon as she came in. He was small, broad and straight-backed, with very short hair, dark beginning to grey. His face was a deep red-brown, and his eyes were inky black and bright. A perfectly trimmed moustache bristled above his smile.

'Charlie, is it?'

'Chalky?'

'That's right. How do you do?'

Without thinking about it Charlie hugged him, and he hugged her back. He patted her gently on her shoulder. 'Will you sit down?' he said. 'Something to drink?'

'No, nothing, thank you. Oh alright, a glass of water.'

Chalky asked the landlord for two.

Now he sat across the table from her, and leaned towards her.

'Well now,' he said, 'have I ever heard a lot about you.'

His eyes actually twinkled. Charlie smiled with embarrassment.

'I don't want to make you feel awkward, but to hear Jase tell it, you are a genius, an artist, a sex bomb, and the most beautiful woman in the entire world, bar none. And an absolute

77

sweetheart. And you're from Wigan.'

'I am from Wigan...' Charlie said cautiously. She realised she had not been so happy for months.

'That man never told me a lie in his life,' Chalky said. 'I can see it's all true. I've read your novel, by the way. Jase made me. It's brilliant.'

'He read it? You – read it to him?'

'Ah, so you knew.'

'Yes.' She nodded. 'I worked it out.'

'I told him you knew.'

'Did he mind?'

'He didn't mind anything to do with you.'

As he said this, Chalky reached out. Ever so gently, he took both her hands in his.

Charlie felt the world break. She refused to believe it, could not believe it, was sure she could not believe it and it would not be true. Not really. But she felt it breaking.

'Is he dead?' she heard herself say.

'Charlie, now listen to me. We don't know. Some people think so, but we don't know. I believe he is alive.'

Charlie stared at him. She thought she was going to faint.

'Drink,' Chalky said, suddenly, and her glass was in her hand and he was guiding it towards her mouth.

'Please just tell me what happened.'

'Ok. Some of the lads were on a job. They got compromised.'

'When was this?'

'New Year's Day.'

'Only ten days ago!'

'Yes.'

'Where?'

'Syria. We were sent in to help these lads. We got them all out. There wasn't enough room in the helicopter so four of us had to wait for the next one. We got hit. There were a lot of them. We were in a messy bit of desert, lots of rocks. Jase went off to flank them – he moved about fifty metres to my left and

78

worked his way forward, and attacked them. Made a complete mess of their plan. Saved us. Saved me. But the other two lads were both hit, one badly. When the heli came I got them on it. By this time he wasn't shooting anymore. Either his weapon jammed, or he ran out of ammo, so he pulled back, or he was lying quiet, letting them go past him, or he was hit. Either way, they were coming in from where he had been, and it was either leave or lose everyone. I was for staying, but the heli wasn't, and I needed to try to keep this lad who was hit alive. So we left him.'

Charlie had withdrawn her hands. She was looking at the table.

'I know,' Chalky said.

'You had to leave,' she said.

'Three lives instead of one, he would say. The other lad lived. And the heli survived, and we all got back. Except Jase, who saved all of us. And I wish to God it had been me, not him. I should have jumped out and gone to find him. He would have done. I should have stayed.'

Charlie looked up sharply now. Chalky was trying to smile at her, but all she could see in his eyes was terrible pain.

'No,' she said. 'Jase only thought of his men. He would have done what you did. The right thing.'

'I tell myself that every minute and it makes no difference,' Chalky said slowly. 'It actually makes it worse.'

'He's dead, isn't he?'

Chalky shook his head. 'Sometimes I hope so. They're a bunch of bastards. Sometimes I know he isn't. It was dark. We had night vision equipment, they didn't. Jase is in great shape, and he's a natural in the desert. He actually likes it. Says it reminds him of Ogmore. I never heard him get hit, never had any sense of it. You tend to know when someone stops one. One minute he was shooting, the next he was gone. Properly gone. I think he worked out that he couldn't make it back to us and bugged out. I'd put my life on it.'

Charlie flinched at the phrase. She wanted to cry and hug

79

Chalky, and she wanted to hit him. She took breaths.

'Shouldn't you be looking for him? Satellites, drones, surely…?'

'They have been and they haven't found him. The thing that makes me most sure he's out there is the bad guys haven't said a word. A body or a prisoner would be gold to them. It would be everywhere. But there's been nothing. So he's out there, somewhere, making his way back.'

'What can we do to help him? There must be something we can do!'

'They're looking for him and they're looking out for him. He'll head for Turkey. Once he gets across he's safe.'

'Do the Turks know he's coming?'

'I asked that – no straight answer. I don't think they trust the Turks, so probably not.'

'So … we … wait?'

'It's the worst thing,' Chalky said, 'for all of us. But yes.'

Charlie took out her phone. Her fingers flew over it.

'Is there somewhere you have to be?' he asked.

'Turkey,' she said. 'There's a flight to Ankara this evening.'

'You are bloody kidding!'

'I am bloody not.'

'But you can't go on your own!'

'I won't be,' Charlie said. She glanced down at her belly, and then at Chalky, and he saw a dark green fire in her eyes. 'I'm going with Jase's daughter. And we'll bring him back. You'll see.'

Luminary

by R.S. Thomas

My luminary,
my morning and evening
star. My light at noon
when there is no sun
and the sky lowers. My balance
of joy in a world
that has gone off joy's
standard. Yours the face
that young I recognised
as though I had known you
of old. Come, my eyes
said, out into the morning
of a world whose dew
waits for your footprint.
Before a green altar
with the thrush for priest
I took those gossamer
vows that neither the Church
could stale nor the Machine
tarnish, that with the years
have grown hard as flint,
lighter than platinum
on our ringless fingers.

Rugby Dads

Jos Andrews

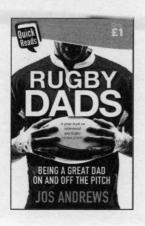

A 2016 Quick Read

From

Accent Press

Code Black

Tom Anderson

The true story of the daredevils who took on the force of nature ... and won

Winter 2013-14: six of the most enormous storms ever to show up in the North Atlantic slammed in to the UK. As buildings fell and valleys flooded, one group of maverick Welsh surfers tackled the sea head-on.

Code Black tells the story of how the Welsh surf scene made history during two months in which conditions made their country rival Hawaii – apart from the cold.

Captain Courage

Gareth Thomas

Be the person you want to be

Gareth Thomas is one of Wales' greatest rugby players known for his speed, powerful physique, fearless attitude and his trademark 'Ayatollah' celebration after scoring a try.

After years of hiding the truth, Gareth became the first international rugby player to come out as gay. He now uses his experience to help others overcome their own problems through his anti-bullying work with school children.

In *Captain Courage* he talks about his life and gives practical tips on how you can be the person you want to be.

For more information about **Quick Reads**

and other **Accent Press** titles

please visit

<u>www.accentpress.co.uk</u>